M000290333

COMING *Back*

A WINDSOR FALLS NOVEL

Kimberley O'Malley (signature)

KIMBERLEY O'MALLEY

Carolina Blue
PUBLISHING

WHERE ROMANCE IS TRUE BLUE & RED HOT!

Published by Carolina Blue Publishing, LLC

Copyright 2019, Carolina Blue Publishing, LLC

ISBN: 978-1-946682-18-5

For all those who have loved and lost. And dared to love again.

"I hold it true, whatever befall; I feel it, when I sorrow most:
'Tis better to have loved and lost Than never to have loved at all."
-Lord Alfred Tennyson

PRAISE FOR
KIMBERLEY O'MALLEY

Coming Home

"There was so much emotion in the story that you will definitely need to keep a box of tissues close by. I felt the heartache, joy, and love that the characters were feeling throughout the story. The author writes a beautiful story that kept me hooked until the end."

–Alpha Book Club

"Kimberley O'Malley really manages to captivate the reader with her words and descriptions. I felt their heartache and joy and loved the ups and downs."

–Texas Book Nook Blog

Taking Chances

"A wonderful witty sarcastic banter love story that shows you that patience and understanding are rewarded and taking risks is worth it in the end when it comes to love."

-Books Are Love

"Ms. O'Malley has a fan for life. Older characters, plots that actually make sense, smexy times, family, characters that you fall in love with, realistic dialogue, perfect pacing, interesting jobs, but above all...LOVE, LAUGHTER, and LIFE. You'll regret it if you don't pick it up."

-Harlie's Book Blog

Second Chances

"This was a good read. Not easy, because it has lots of emotional topics, but it grabs the reader into it. I have truly enjoyed the writing style of Ms. O'Malley and I really look forward to read more from her."

-More Books Than Livros Blog

"Second chances should all be so sweet...I love this series and the characters that inhabit it! Drama and turmoil stirs up this small town and gives these relatable characters an extra snap to their step."

-Nerdy, Dirty, & Flirty Book Blog

Saving Quinn

"This was my first read by this author and I was blown away by this book! The characters, the story line... Everything was just perfect! I loved the characters they were just amazing. Paige is a Kindergarten teacher and Quinn is a firefighter. I don't have the words to do justice with this review! and I certainly don't wanna give anything away. So, I'm gonna end this by saying YOU HAVE TO READ THIS BOOK!!!"

-Under Covers Book Blog

"I love the Windsor Falls series. This one was just as good as the last three. It made me laugh and cry. I love how Kimberly O' Malley puts so many real-life situations into her stories."

-A. Fleming, Amazon customer

"Nobody brings the heat more than a sexy fireman. And trust me, Saving Quinn is one sexy read!! I absolutely loved Paige and Quinn. You are instantly drawn into this story, the characters and their lives!!! This is a book that I will look forward to rereading again and again!!!!

-Shauntelle B., Amazon customer

Finding Kat

"Another winning entry to the Windsor Falls Series. A lovely, heartfelt book with wonderfully complex characters and storyline. Kat and Sebastian are wonderful, they have amazing chemistry, and a really great connection that builds throughout the book. It's lovely to catch up with earlier characters as well."

-Book Addict Studio

"I flipping loved this book! Kat and Sebastian are everything!!!Sebastian was thinking he was done with women... until he met Kat! Sparks fly with these 2. I'm not gonna spoil anything so I'm stopping! But everyone needs to read this book!"

-Ashely Sledge, Under Covers Book Blog

"This was such an enjoyable read. The combination of great characters, heart-warming storyline and emotions that locked me in from the opening pages. With each chapter Kat's journey from family traditions to standing up for what she wants and believes in, got stronger and stronger. Throw in a sexy cardiologist and you get the perfect read."

-Nicki Holt, The Overflowing Bookcase

Chapter One

Amy Windsor pulled the collar of her coat higher around her neck, steeling herself from the bitter wind sweeping across the cemetery. Nothing could warm her frozen heart. She walked slowly, forcing her feet to take each, next step. If she didn't see the name of her dead fiancé on his tombstone, maybe it wasn't real. Of course, she knew he was dead. Had attended his firefighter funeral almost eighteen months ago. Yet some days, it still didn't seem real. Some days, she almost forgot. Some days, she awoke with the peace of knowing he lay next to her. Until she remembered. Until her hand discovered the empty space next to her.

She'd made it through a year of firsts; first Christmas without him, first birthday without him, first anniversary of his death. People assured her time healed all wounds. People lied. Or forgot to mention how breathing became difficult without him. How her chest felt empty, as though he had literally taken her heart with him. Another Christmas approached, with Thanksgiving barely survived. And still, she waited to feel something different. Anything. Since she stood at this very site, in the blazing July heat last year, she'd waited to feel something other than the endless emptiness.

Weeks, months really, had passed since she last visited. In the beginning, when she'd first lost him, Amy came daily. She sat on the ground near his grave, staring but not seeing. Trying to understand how this had happened to him. To them. She brought flowers. She cleaned his headstone. Anything to make her feel closer to him. But nothing worked. The visits only left her sadder. She stopped coming as often, staying in her room instead. No doubt worrying her family and best friend. But she hadn't known what else to do. How to move forward without Andrew. The life they'd planned, getting married and starting a family, all disappeared in the blink of an eye, leaving her behind.

She clutched the holly sprigs like a lifeline. Andrew wasn't here in this place. The hole in the ground held only his body, not the essence of what made him special. Where it had gone was anyone's guess. She'd believed in many things before his untimely line of duty death. Now, not so much. Now, she put one foot in front of the other. And waited for her life to begin again. Or maybe to be over.

A man's voice, low and husky, broke her thoughts. It held a familiar ring. She glanced around but didn't see anyone. She disliked coming upon other grieving friends and family. Their open displays of grief left her hollow. She would give anything to cry. But it hadn't happened since Quinn Adams, her best friend's boyfriend, broke the news of Andrew's death. She remembered screaming at Quinn to not tell her what she already knew. What she realized the second she looked into his red-rimmed eyes. The love of her life was gone. Andrew had only ever broken one promise to her, that he would always find a way to come home to her.

Straightening to her just shy of six feet, Amy shook off the thought. *It didn't help. Best to get this over with.* Tightening the belt of her coat, she skirted a snow-covered tree and came to a halt at the sight of a man hunkered down before Andrew's grave. She could hear him speaking but was far enough away to not make out the actual words.

Stepping back, she snapped a dry branch under her foot, catching the man's attention. He rose in one graceful movement, turning toward her as he did. They both froze, almost as if held in place by the chilly wind whipping around them. Less than a hundred yards apart, the shocking red hair gave away his identity. Travis Mac Gregor, better known as Mac. A local paramedic and friend of Quinn's, he had also been one of the last people to see Andrew alive. She turned and fled.

"Wait. Please, Amy, wait a minute."

She stopped in her tracks, staring at the pristine snow around her boot-clad feet. Not because she wanted to. Every cell in her body screamed for her to run. Get to her car and drive far away from here. But she stood still and waited for him to reach her. Her breath, ragged at best, formed a fog in front of her face. She felt him approach but didn't turn.

"I'm sorry. I didn't realize anyone else would be here today. I'll go."

He walked around her, careful to not touch her. Her fault.

She reached out a hand toward his retreating back. "Mac, wait," she called in a small, voice.

He halted, paused, and then turned to face her. His green eyes held more than a hint of unease. Also, her fault. He'd tried to speak with her several times since Andrew's death, starting at the funeral, but she'd always refused, walking away. She didn't even know why. He had stopped trying a while ago.

She tilted her head to look into those eyes as she addressed him. She shoved her hands deep into her coat pockets. *No need for him to see them shake.* "What were you saying to him?" She'd meant to apologize for her less than polite behavior these past months, but curiosity got the better of her.

His face reddened, whether from the question or the cold, she didn't know. He blew on his hands for a moment. "Oh, nothing much. Told him how much I skinned Flynn at last week's poker game." A grin broke out across his handsome face. "He would have loved it."

She stared at him, not quite knowing what to think. "Oh. Okay." Amy stomped her feet, trying to warm them. She tilted her head, peering at him. "That might be the very last thing I expected to hear."

He shrugged his shoulders. "I don't come here often. Not anymore. I don't want to, uh, anyway, I'm not sure why I even did today. Maybe the holidays made me do it." He stared at a point over her shoulder. "It's not like he's here. I talk to him from time to time, wherever I am when the impulse takes hold."

She bit her bottom lip. "You don't come here anymore because of me. Is that what you were trying so hard to not say?" She exhaled as he squirmed. "Also, my fault, and I'm sorry."

He took a slow step toward her, almost tentative, and shook his head. "I don't blame you for not wanting to talk to me. I'm sure I only bring back bad memories. You don't need it."

Her smile grew tight. "Don't lose sleep over it. They're never very far away." She drew her hands from her warm pockets and tucked her hair behind her ears. "I've treated you badly. And I am sorry. It was easier, somehow, to not talk with you. My mother would skin me alive if she knew. She raised me better."

The smile forming on his face fell. "Well, I won't take any more of your time." He turned back toward the grave, skirting it, before disappearing down the hill.

She heard, rather than saw, him drive away. When the sound disappeared, Amy approached Andrew's grave. She placed the holly at the base of the marble headstone. Brushing snow off the small, stone bench near it, she sat, allowing the cold to seep through to bones. *Andrew Daniel Jefferson, September 14, 1985-July 20, 2017, Beloved Son, Devoted Fiancé, Dedicated Firefighter; the world is darker without you.* She'd read the words more times than she could recall, traced them with her fingers in the beginning. But she'd never spoken to him here as Mac had.

Andrew remained with her, in her heart, wherever she went. In the beginning, she dreamt of him. Vivid dreams which left her empty and aching when she awoke only to realize they were not real. She'd lie in bed in the early morning, clutching a pillow, wishing it was him she held. But he wasn't coming home to her. They wouldn't be given a second chance.

Paige Harrington, one day to be Paige Adams if she ever set a wedding date, urged Amy to go back to teaching. The two had been born within weeks of each other and inseparable ever since. Until Andrew died. Paige was the sister she never had, and she missed their closeness. But Paige had gone on with her life, while Amy stayed frozen in time. She missed her best friend. She missed having lunch with her at work. Most of all, she missed the closeness of a person who could finish her sentences. There was a time when they never went a day without talking to each other, let alone multiple times per day. Another casualty of Andrew's death. Another thing she'd caused.

She'd be hard-pressed to say what exactly she'd done for the past year and a half. Mostly just survived. The sad truth was nothing felt right anymore. Her skin felt as though it didn't quite fit her. On some level, this worried her. But what healed a shattered heart?

*****

Mac drove through town, jaw clenched, not sure where he was going. He ended up at Town Hall and pulled into a visitor spot. He was off today and had time to kill. Maybe he could talk his friend, Quinn Adams, into a late lunch or early dinner. Taking a moment to chill, he thought about seeing Amy. *What was it about her that always set his teeth on edge?* Windsor Falls, N.C. was a small town. Everyone pretty much knew each other since birth. He had graduated with her older brother, Alex. It didn't make them buddies, though.

Alex and Amy were Windsors, as in Windsor Falls. Their great, great God knew how many grandfathers founded the town. He was a Mac Gregor, which didn't mean anything to anyone. Alex had been, probably still was, very caught up in it all. Amy probably was too. He knew *of* her rather than actually knew her. But then everyone here knew of Amy. Besides being a member of the founding family, she was almost six feet tall with blonde hair and bright green eyes. If she wasn't a Windsor, she could easily be a famous model or actress. But Windsors didn't pursue careers beneath them.

He'd been trying to talk to her ever since her fiancé died last year. Mac had been unlucky enough to be working that fateful day. He closed his eyes on the memory of watching the life slip away from his friend. Quinn had ridden in the ambulance with A. J., talking to him until his friend lost consciousness. The dying firefighter's last words had been about Amy. They haunted him to this day. He wanted, needed maybe, to tell her. But she would never let him.

Today had caught him off guard. After being rebuffed by her several times, he'd given up trying. He'd even stopped visiting A.J.'s grave, not wanting to take the chance of running into her. Words failed him when she called his name softly. It might not have been the ideal place, standing in the freezing cold cemetery, but Mac really wanted to tell her about the last conversation. Then she'd brought up 'being raised better than that' and he remembered. She didn't need anything from a Mac Gregor.

Muscles tensing, Mac got out of his pickup. No use dwelling on things he couldn't change, as his Granny Mac Gregor always used to say. She'd be twirling in her grave if she could see him worrying what a Windsor thought. Shaking off his mood, he walked through the front door of the municipal building.

Quinn, who had been a firefighter for over a decade when A.J. died, now worked in the county arson squad. Not wanting to return to the fire service after his best friend's death, he had instead taken up this cause. His first big case had been finding the bastard who set the fatal fire. He shook his head at what people would do for money. The abandoned warehouse had been worth more in insurance than sitting empty.

He opened the arson investigation office door and smiled at Debbie, the young woman who served as the department secretary. "Hey, Debbie. Is Quinn in?"

He tried to ignore the blush crawling up the woman's cheeks at the sight of him. She couldn't be more than twenty-two, which was more than a decade younger than him. And triple that in life experience. Debbie still lived at home with her parents who would be horrified at the idea of their precious baby dating him.

"Oh, hi, Mac, I mean Mr. Mac Gregor. Quinn is, uh, on the phone, I think. Would you like to take a seat? I'm sure he'll be right with you."

"Sure, thanks." He sank into the less than comfortable visitor chair and tried to avoid direct eye contact with her. She was a sweet kid, but the last thing he wanted was to encourage her crush. He picked up a magazine and thumbed through it, pretending to be interested in golf of all things. This was worse than his doctor's office. They at least had Sports Illustrated.

He stood as Quinn's door opened, thankful he hadn't been long. "Hey, man, are you up for some lunch?"

Quinn motioned him inside his office. "Sure, give me a second. I have to send one more email." He followed Mac inside, closing the door behind him. Once behind the desk, he tapped quickly on his laptop.

"Thank you," Mac whispered. "I couldn't stay out there one more second."

Quinn covered a laugh, shaking a finger at his friend. "Why don't you ask her out already? You know she likes you. And it's not like you have a line of women waiting. Eventually, Paige is going to let me set a wedding date. What are you going to do, come stag?"

"I know she likes me. Everyone in town knows she likes me." He rubbed a hand along the back of his neck. "I think she may have been doodling her first name with my last."

Quinn lost it then, laughing until his face turned red.

"Some friend you are," Mac muttered, waiting for Quinn to get it under control.

"I, uh, I am your friend," he squeaked out, still laughing and wiping at his eyes.

"Then find me someone. I'm tired of being single. I'm tired of first dates from Hell. I'm tired of all my friends getting engaged or married or having babies and leaving me in the dust."

It was true. Poker night had gone from one married guy, Donovan Fitzgerald, to what seemed like only a few single guys left. Flynn was back from his destination wedding only a few weeks. Brendan was engaged to Charlie, one of the ER doctors he liked working with. Sam and Elizabeth, his other favorite ER doctor, married last fall and had an almost six-month-old son, Gabriel Connor. Quinn, of course, had Paige and would marry her tomorrow if she would finally agree to set a date.

"When are you and Paige going to tie the knot? Is she getting cold feet?" He drew himself up to his full height, six feet, five inches, and puffed out his chest. "I'd be happy to step in," he offered, tongue planted firmly in cheek.

His friend didn't laugh as he had hoped but sank into his desk chair, raking a hand through his short, blonde hair. "You know I'd have married her yesterday if she'd agree." He let out a sigh. "But she won't until Amy is 'in a better place,' whatever that means."

"Because they're best friends?" He knew the two had been inseparable from birth, even working together. Until last year and A.J.'s death. Still, Paige shouldn't be expected to put her life on hold. Neither should Quinn.

"Amy hasn't gotten over losing A.J. And I feel terrible saying this, but I need to move on. He was my best friend, long before she ever knew him." He stopped and shook his head. "That came out all wrong. Those two fell in love the moment they met. I was there, saw the whole thing with my own two eyes. He talked about marrying her within hours of meeting her. Mind you, I thought he was crazy. But he wasn't.

They were good for each other. And I know she's hurting. I can't imagine what I would do if I lost Paige." His brown eyes darkened as if the very thought was too painful to behold.

Mac cleared his throat, looking for the right words. "But his dying isn't your fault. And you have the right to move on with your life. As you said, you knew A.J. for years. He was your best friend."

Quinn waved a hand between them. "It's fine. I asked her to marry me, and she said yes. We don't want a big wedding anyway, so we can plan something on the spur of the moment. Paige will let me know when the time is right."

"You could always jet off to Saint Lucia like Flynn and Katie did. Sounds like a fun way to do it. And, even better, the guys didn't have to wear monkey suits," joked Mac.

Quinn stood. "What a great idea. When the time comes, I'll have to mention it to Paige. Now, didn't you mention lunch? I'm starving."

Mac followed him out of his office, avoiding eye contact with Debbie as he left. No use making it harder on her. Or him. He thought about Amy and how she was inadvertently holding up Quinn's wedding. He wondered if she knew. Or if she even cared.

Chapter Two

Amy glanced at Paige attempting a Downward Facing Dog position. She gave her maybe a moment before she fell flat on her face. In an endless series of attempts to drag her kicking and screaming back to the real world, fitness was a bold choice. Despite perpetually moaning about her 'last twenty pounds,' her best friend had never been any good at physical exercise. She hated running and swore the gym made her break out in hives. She must be desperate. Paige had thrown out the idea of a yoga class. Amy had one-upped her, opting for hot yoga.

She watched as Paige landed in a sweaty pile and held in a laugh, resisting a 'told you so.' She was lucky to have her. Even luckier Paige hadn't given up on her yet. Others had. The so-called friends who couldn't handle her being a grieving widow. Well, not quite a widow. She never got the chance to be a wife. At first, there had really been too much attention. There were mounds of flowers and cards, the former she'd donated to a local nursing home. Better someone enjoy them. She wasn't going to. Then the calls, texts, and emails dwindled. She couldn't blame them. Amy hadn't answered a single one. But Paige hadn't given up on her. Even on her darkest days, when she railed at her friend for checking on her after not answering a phone call or text, Paige never stopped caring. Never stopped trying to draw Amy out again.

Taking pity on her best friend, Amy rolled up her mat and stood. "Let's blow this popsicle stand," she whispered to a flushed Paige.

"What?" Paige glanced around at the other yoga students and lowered her voice. "I was getting the hang of it."

"No, you weren't. But I love you for trying." Amy walked around the other students in their row and headed to the locker rooms. Once inside, a relieved Paige collapsed on a bench.

"Oh, shish kebob, it was horrible."

She sat there, dripping sweat and panting, making Amy laugh. It might have felt a bit rusty but good none the less. "I know you worry about me, Paige. But hot yoga is clearly not the answer."

"Agreed. How about some ice cream? It always makes me feel better."

Chocolate marshmallow wouldn't fill the empty space in her heart, but if it made Paige happy, then it was worth it. "Sure. My treat. Give me a few minutes to change." She turned to the locker she had chosen on the way in and grabbed her bag. "Luckily, I barely broke a sweat. I'll throw on some deodorant."

Paige, now lying on the bench, arms akimbo, muttered, "I may hate you," between breaths.

"No, you don't, Paige Harrington. You love me. Don't think I don't know and appreciate it either." A lump rose in her throat, and she turned away to gather herself. She had no idea what might have happened to her if not for Paige and her family. There had been many days where Amy had welcomed the oblivion of sleep. Probably too many.

A sweaty Paige got off the bench and hugged her from behind. "That's what best friends do. They love you. And they hold on and don't let go."

"And I appreciate it." Amy wrinkled her nose. "But right now, you're a bit ripe."

Paige sniffed under her arms, making a face. "Oops,

sorry. Let me freshen up a bit before we go." She grinned. "Somehow, I didn't think hot yoga would be quite this hot. Who knew?"

"I did, silly goose. I warned you."

"I suppose."

Amy finished dressing as her best friend made herself more presentable. She glanced in the mirror and grimaced at her hair. What had once been shiny and vibrant now hung limp and lackluster around her face. She tried to remember when the last time she'd visited the hair salon but couldn't. *Probably not a good sign.* What else had she neglected? Examining herself more closely in the mirror, Amy shuddered. Her clothes hung on her. She was tall for a woman, just shy of six feet, and had the natural metabolism of a toddler. It drove Paige crazy. Maintaining a healthy weight had never been a problem. But now she looked gaunt and pale.

When was the last time food held any appeal? Andrew would not be happy with her. She'd been sleepwalking through life for the past year and a half. It was long past time to stop. But where to begin? Ice cream seemed like as good a place as any.

Paige appeared next to her in the mirror. "What are we looking at?" she asked.

Amy shook her head. "A wreck."

Paige wrapped her arm around her, pulling her in to her side. "Not a wreck. Just someone who needs a little something."

Amy barked out a sarcastic laugh and picked up a chunk of her lifeless hair. "Be honest with me. Look at this. I haven't had my hair cut or anything since-" She stopped short, not completing her sentence.

"Since A.J. died. You can say it, Amy. It doesn't make it any more real than it already is." She turned to face her. "Get a haircut. Or a pedi. Do something fun. Andrew would not want you living this way. This would break his heart. He loved you, Amy."

She sucked in a sharp breath, her heart throbbing. "You may be psychic. I was just thinking the same thing. He would be unhappy with me. It's honestly the first time this has even occurred to me." She dropped her gaze to the floor.

"It's a good sign, right? Caring about stuff again." Paige clapped her hands together. "Ooh, there are so many things you can do. Let's make a list." She turned and rooted in her purse.

Amy put her hand on Paige's arm, stopping her. "Let's not go crazy. I need time to get going again." She smiled at Paige's frown. "Not another year, mind you, but I should ease myself back into things. Back into life."

"Does this mean you'll go back to the support group at the hospital?"

She hated to squash Paige's puppy-like enthusiasm, but on this she would stand firm. The other group members had at least twenty years on her. Others even more. One woman had sobbed openly about her husband. When Amy realized he'd been dead for more than a decade, she left the room. And never went back. Not even Paige could make her go back. Her own grief paralyzed her at times. Theirs was a burden she couldn't stand.

"No, don't think I'll be going back. I was thinking about seeing what Jamie had on grief, though." Their mutual friend owned the local bookstore, Between the Covers. She sponsored their monthly book club, yet another thing Amy had skipped for a long time. While she loved to read, she'd lost the attention span for it.

"I'll take it." Paige gathered up her bag and purse. "I'm ready if you are. I wonder what the flavor of the day is."

The two women left the yoga studio, debating the merits of various flavors. They walked the two blocks to Iced Bliss. The locally owned store served freshly made ice cream and gelato. They had limited hours in the winter but still had a faithful year-round following. Paige held the door as the two women entered.

"Wow, I've never seen it this empty," she marveled.

"Well, it is thirty degrees outside."

They made their way to the counter as the owner, an older man named Barry, appeared from the back room.

"Afternoon, ladies. What can I get you? We have a limited menu this time of year, but there are plenty of delicious choices."

Amy watched as her friend perused the options. Watching Paige decide on ice cream was amusing.

Paige bit her lip. "I don't know if I can choose between Chocolate Cherry Lover and Fudge Surprise."

"Who says you have to choose, pretty lady?"

Paige blushed. "I failed at hot yoga. The last thing I need is two scoops."

"Okay then, how about a smaller scoop of both? Does that work for you?"

"Oh, all right. You sold me. But make sure those are really smaller scoops."

"Coming right up. I'll get yours next, Miss."

"I'm still deciding anyway." She looked at the list again. The dozen choices highlighted another of her problems, making decisions. Maybe she should close her eyes and point. The bell over the door rang, breaking her concentration. She turned to see Mac enter the small shop. *Great! Just what she needed.* She'd already made a fool of herself in front of him this week.

"Hey, Mac," called Paige as she accepted her ice cream cone. "Haven't seen you in a while. How've you been?"

Amy watched as the other woman rushed over to hug the huge man. It was a comical sight. He had to have over a foot on her. She turned back to the freezer case as Barry approached her. "I'll have the Party Hardy Cake," she blurted out. Pleased she'd decided, she moved closer to the cash register to pay, not to mention get out of his path. She could feel his eyes on her.

"I'll take a single dip of Not Your Grandmother's Vanilla, Barry. And I've got these." He reached in his pocket for his wallet as Amy protested.

"It's not necessary." She hated the way her voice shook, but he made her feel like an idiot. She couldn't let him pay for her ice cream.

"I think I can handle it," he responded in a tone barring any debate.

She turned toward him, taking in his paramedic uniform. "Well, then, thank you." At least she had managed to say it without tripping over her tongue. *What was it about him?*

He frowned down at her. "Wasn't so hard, now was it?"

Now it was her turn to frown. His tone left icicles in the air between them. What had she done this time? She accepted her cone from Barry and joined Paige at a table. "Are you happy with your choices?"

Mid lick, she grinned. "I'm always happy with ice cream, as you know. Probably a little too happy. I should probably take up running again."

"Again? When did you ever run?"

"Well, here and there." She threw up her hands. "Oh, all right, I've never actually run more than a block without thinking I would die. Doesn't mean I can't start. Maybe if I work up to it."

"I think you look fine the way you are, Paige. I'm sure your fiancé would agree if he was here," added Mac.

Amy watched as he pulled over a chair to their cozy little table for two. So much for him leaving as she had hoped. "Of course, she is. She's more than 'fine.' Paige is beautiful."

One red eyebrow rose. "I already said that. Why do you make it sound like I didn't?"

Really? How had they gotten into this inane conversation? She didn't want to talk to him about anything, let alone this. "Paige is beautiful and doesn't have to worry about her weight, even though she does."

"Good. Then we agree. I thought maybe Paige was worried because she's engaged. My partner, Trina, went a little crazy with her diet while she was wedding dress shopping. I almost had to start an IV on her to keep her hydrated."

Paige gasped softly. Her hand shook, causing chocolate to splatter on her shirt. "Oh, I'm a mess. I'm going to run in the bathroom and try to fix this." She left the table before Amy could follow. Instead, she whirled on Mac.

"Nice going," she all but snarled.

Seemingly unaffected by her anger, he took a large bite of his cone with even, white teeth. After swallowing, he deigned to reply. "And how exactly is this *my* fault? All I did was mention her engagement. Quinn is a good friend of mine."

"They haven't even set a date yet, if you must know. I'm sure she hasn't even thought about a wedding dress."

He leaned in closer, taking all the oxygen with him. "And why do you think it is, Amy?" His voice was soft but firm. He never broke eye contact. "Something to think about." He stood and left before she could respond.

She stared at his retreating back, grinding her teeth. What was wrong with him? Maybe she had been right to avoid speaking with him. Of all the terrible things to say. And then the reality of his words hit her like a ton of bricks. *Had Paige not set a date because of her?*

The woman in question returned from the bathroom, wet spot on her shirt. She glanced around the shop. "Where did Mac go?"

"I think he had to get back to work. He didn't say." Guilt boiled inside her. She needed to clear the air with Paige but now wasn't the time.

Paige shrugged. "Too bad. I was going to see if he wanted to come to dinner one night next week. There's a new teacher I think he might like."

Amy zoned out as Paige went on about the new teacher and her first ever attempt at matchmaking. The thought of her best friend putting her life on hold because of her became a rock in the pit of her stomach. She hoped it wasn't true. But Paige rarely brought up anything about her engagement with Amy.

She stood. "I'm kind of tired. Do you mind if I go home now?" She cringed at the look of hurt flashing across Paige's face, but she had to leave. The walls closed in on her. She needed air. Grabbing her coat, she kissed Paige's cheek before leaving the shop. "I'll call you," she threw over her shoulder before all but running outside.

Amy hurried around the corner, stopping out of sight in an alley. She stood with her forehead against the cold brick of a building, grounding herself. She waited until her heart settled back into a normal rate. *What had she done?* All this time, Paige never said a word to her. She really was a horrible best friend. She needed to fix this.

*****

Mac strode into the paramedic building, banging the door shut as he went. His partner, Trina, looked up from her magazine. "Ice cream not agree with you? I told you it's too cold outside."

"It's not the cold bothering me," he ground out. Mac paced the length of the crew room, trying to work off some steam. What was it about her making him nuts? Where would he even start? She was too rich, too blonde, too perfect. The last thought stopped him in his tracks. *Where had that thought come from?* He dropped onto the couch, trying to ignore the curious stare from his partner.

It didn't work. She knew him too well. This wasn't a normal mood for him.

"What?"

She closed the magazine she'd been reading, tossing it on the pile of others on the coffee table. "I have no idea. But it's very amusing whatever crawled up your ass and died."

"Gee, thanks," he all but growled at her.

"Careful before your face freezes this way," she teased him. When it didn't improve his mood, she frowned. "Okay, now you have to tell me. You're not a door slammer."

Her comment made him smile. "You're right. Slamming doors is more your speed." His tiny partner blamed her Latina heritage every time she slammed a door.

"Exactly. What's up with you?" After crossing her arms over her chest, Trina settled in to wait him out.

He groaned. She wasn't one to back down. Ever. "I had another run in with Amy Windsor, if you must know." Wonderful, now he sounded like a petulant toddler.

She clucked her tongue at him. He hated when she did it. It inevitably meant she was right about something.

"Spit it out. You know you want to."

"I should have known it was about her. No one else twists you. What did she do this time?"

He replayed the conversation at the ice cream parlor. He couldn't wait to hear her response. She always had his back. But she sat there, shaking her head instead.

"What?"

"You said that? To Amy? What's wrong with you?"

He shot up off the couch to resume pacing. "Why are you taking her side? You're my partner."

"You basically told a woman whose whole life was ripped out from under her she was being selfish. Really, Mac? I'm not taking sides, but it was a terrible thing to say to her."

His stomach sank. "But, it's true," he protested weakly. "Paige won't let Quinn set a wedding date until Amy is 'back on her feet.' His words not mine."

"Paige and Amy have been friends since their mothers were pregnant together. Everyone knows it, Mac. She had this fabulous whirlwind romance with A.J., got engaged, only to have him die. Did you know they were looking through wedding magazines for dresses when the story broke on the local news?"

Acid slithered through his gut like a poisonous snake. His face must have given something away.

"What? What else have you done?"

"I, uh, may have mentioned wedding dresses." He sat down, hard, and hung his head. "In my defense, I had no idea," he muttered to no one in particular.

"You have to apologize to her. I know you, Mac. You wouldn't deliberately hurt a fly. What is it about her?"

"I have no idea." He had an inkling, but he wasn't telling his partner. He'd never live it down. This week kept getting worse. She was right. He owed Amy an apology. It didn't mean he had to be happy about it. He needed to avoid her at all costs in the future.

*****

The interior of Between the Covers never failed to cheer Amy. Today was no different. The soft blues and greens on the walls and furnishings created a comfortable environment inviting visitors to linger. Jamie was a smart businesswoman. The warmth today also helped. She stepped inside, pulling the door closed on the chilly wind picking up outside. There would be more snow tonight.

"Amy," the owner cried as she rounded the counter. Jamie pulled her into her arms, hugging her. She really needed to get out more often if people were this happy to see her.

When Jamie let her go, Amy smiled at her. "I've missed you, too."

"I don't see you in here enough. And everyone from book club misses you." The gentle reproach hit its intended mark.

"I know. I miss them as well. I ordered every book through your website. I, uh, have a hard time committing to anything right now."

Jamie's very expressive face fell. "Oh, I'm sorry. I wasn't trying to make you feel badly. We just miss you. How have you been?"

She blew out a breath and unzipped her coat. "I have good days and bad, I guess. I need your help."

Jamie squeezed her hand. "Anything for you."

"I was hoping you might be able to suggest some books on grief. I need to get my life back. This thing I've been doing, the staying in and pretending life isn't passing me by, isn't working."

"Of course, I have something for you. Let's look in the

self-help section. And for what it's worth, Amy, I think you're brave. I don't know what I might do in your situation."

Amy shrugged. "I feel the very opposite of brave. I've been stuck since he died, Jamie. I'm only existing, not really living. And now, I'm tired of myself. Lead the way, please."

"My pleasure, follow me." On the way across the store, Jamie grabbed a novel off a rounder. "This is the current book club selection. Take it home with you. And really try to make the next meeting."

"I will. I promise."

They turned a corner. Halfway down the row, Jamie halted. "It's a small section, but I have some excellent choices. I recommend either of these." She pulled two books from the shelf, handing them to Amy. "But feel free to browse. A couple deal specifically with the death of a spouse." The bell over the door rang. "Excuse me. I'm here alone. I'll be up front if you need me."

Amy watched her bustle to the front and greet a new customer. She took the recommended books and walked to the plush seating in the back of the store. Sinking into an overstuffed chair, she glanced at the back of the first book. Her heart beat wildly as she read. It could have been written about her. This wasn't going to be easy. Not for the first time, Amy considered seeing a therapist. Just because the support group hadn't worked for her didn't mean one on one wouldn't. Alex would be horrified, but she couldn't care less what her brother thought. He cared way too much about being a Windsor in Windsor Falls.

Exhaustion crashed over her. She stood, taking all three books to the counter. She'd attempt to read them when she got home. While waiting for Jamie to finish with a customer, she glanced around the store. She had spent many pleasant evenings here, discussing the merits of various books the club had read. She needed to make the effort to make the next one.

"Did you decide on one?"

She started at Jamie's question. "Oh, sorry. Guess I was lost in thought." She placed all three books on the counter.

"I'll take them all. And I promise to be at the next book club get together. You can tell Paige I said so. She'll make sure I make it."

"Yay, I'm glad. We really do miss you."

"I miss you guys, too." *And my old self.*

Chapter Three

On Friday evening, Amy stood in the town square, stamping her feet to keep them warm, as she waited for the annual tree lighting ceremony to begin. She'd missed this last year. Of course, she'd missed everything in the past eighteen months. Her pulse bounded in her ears. *Don't think about it. Look forward.* Short but effective, the pep talk brought her back to the present. She blew on her hands, wishing she'd remembered to bring gloves.

"Didn't expect to see you here."

No point in turning around. Amy knew the voice. "Good evening, Mac."

He stopped next to her. Without another word, he pulled off his gloves and handed them to her.

She hesitated a moment before reaching out for them. "Thank you. That's very kind."

"More like practical. If you develop frostbite, I'll be forced to act. And I'm off-duty."

"Ah." As usual, she had no idea what to say to him. Before Andrew died, she could hold conversations with anyone at any time. After all, she was a Windsor. She'd been brought up making small talk.

"Is it just me?" he asked in the sultry, night disc jockey voice   of   his.

"Is what just you?" She knew what he was asking but felt the need to buy some time.

"Really?" He shook his head. "Never mind." He turned and left before she could say another word. Or give him back his gloves.

She stared at the dark tree, listening to the chatter of families all around her. Her shoulders slumped. She wasn't ready. Amy left the square, heading for Cup O' Joe, the coffee place next to her friend Kat's bakery.

The bell over the door tinkled her arrival. Sally, wife of Joe from the name, grinned at her from behind the counter. "Amy!" she cried before coming around the counter to enfold Amy in her arms. "It's wonderful to see you, honey. You look fabulous."

"I own a mirror, Sally. I know how much you're stretching the truth." She smiled to soften her words, happy to be here in this shop where she'd spent endless hours. "Where's Joe?"

"Oh, you know my husband. He's out there, in the thick of things, selling hot beverages to the crowd." She grimaced. "Not me. I keep begging him to consider moving to Florida. These old bones are about done with winter."

The thought forced the smile from her lips. The thought of more change put her stomach in a nosedive. "Oh, is it something you're seriously considering?"

"I am. But you know Joe. Not a huge fan of change."

"True," she responded, looking around the shop. Not much had changed since she and Paige first started coming here in high school. "I know it's selfish of me to say, but I'd really miss you guys if you left."

Sally squeezed her hands. "Not much danger of it happening. Now, what can I get you?"

"She'll have a hot chocolate, extra whipped cream. Make it two," answered Paige, coming through the door. "I looked for you outside, Amy."

"I ducked in here for reinforcement against the cold first. We still have a bit of time before the actual lighting."

"Especially if the mayor talks," quipped Sally. "You know how he loves to talk."

Paige rolled her eyes. "He's a good mayor, but you're right. There's nothing he likes better than addressing a crowd."

"Why don't you ladies grab a table, I'll bring these drinks to you in a moment."

"Thanks, Sally." Amy sat at the nearest table, pulling off Mac's gloves as she did.

"New fashion statement?" inquired her best friend.

"What? Oh, these." She nodded at the pair of ridiculously large gloves sitting on the table. "No, Mac lent them to me outside. I'd forgotten mine."

"Mac was here? I didn't see him anywhere."

"He, uh, left." She hid her expression behind the curtain of her hair. She didn't have the heart to tell Paige she'd been rude to him. Again.

"What happened?"

Sally arrived, placing two steaming mugs of hot chocolate before them. "Enjoy, ladies."

Amy wrapped her hands around hers, enjoying the warmth of the heated ceramic.

"Nice try. Don't think I forgot."

"Of course, you didn't." She swirled a spoon through her drink, wondering how to not sound like an idiot. "I don't know what it is about him. Every time I see him, I end up with my foot in my mouth."

"What did you say to him this time?" She couldn't hide the smirk on her face. "Honestly, Amy, everyone else loves him. You, not so much."

"He rubs me the wrong way," she muttered.

"Are you sure?"

She sighed. "He reminds me of what I've lost. He's tried, several times, to approach me, since Andrew died. And I can't. And now I have to return his gloves." She gave the offending items a shove.

"Oh, Amy." Paige reached across the table, placing a hand

over hers.

She meant well, but more sympathy was the last thing Amy needed. "I appreciate the thought. Really, I do. But I need to move on. Get back out there. And I am trying. But he brings it all back. Or brings me back to the day. I'm not sure which. I need to get past it and seeing him is like putting a loop on my life."

"Rome wasn't built in a day, as they say. Give yourself a chance, Amy. Think of all you've done this week alone. You'll find your own ways to break the cycle"

"How did I ever get so lucky to have you as my best friend?"

"Our mothers were best friends and pregnant together probably helped," Paige joked.

"There is that. But seriously, I wouldn't know what to do without you."

"You mean without the nagging?"

Amy smiled. "I stopped by Jaime's the other day. After hot yoga."

"Nice! She must have been thrilled to see you."

"She was, but not half as much as I was to see her. I bought a couple of books on grief. And this month's book club read."

"Woohoo!" she yelled in response, getting up to hug her.

"Breath. I need to breathe," Amy joked in response to her friend's enthusiasm.

Paige plunked down in the chair next to her, eyes overly bright. "This is amazing. I'll stop now."

"Well, if you thought that was amazing, hold on to your hat." She took a deep breath. "I want you and Quinn to set a date. Today."

Paige's mouth formed a perfect O. "Are you sure?"

"More than sure. In my grief, I never thought about how this affected you guys. No more waiting. Life is short. Grab the man and marry him already. And no matter how you choose to do it, I will be there at your side, smiling bigger than anyone else."

Tears streamed down her friend's face. Happy ones at least.

"Oh, my goodness. I have to go." Paige jumped up, toppling over her chair. "I have to find Quinn." She ran out of the store, coat open, hot chocolate long forgotten.

"What in the world?" asked Sally from behind the counter. "She ran out of here like the very devil chased her. Is everything okay?"

Amy grinned at the older woman. "Better than okay. She's getting married."

Sally clapped her hands. "Well, it's about time!"

Amy's grin slipped a bit, knowing for certain she had been the reason for the delay. "Agreed." She finished her drink and paid Sally for both before leaving the store. She pulled on Travis's large, fleece-lined gloves against the bite of the night air. With the sun fully set, the temperature dropped even further.

A chorus of oohs and aahs erupted across the street. She glanced over in time to see the large evergreen burst into light with the flip of a switch. An ache settled in her chest. One more thing Andrew would never share with her.

One step forward. One step to the side.

The following night, Amy stood on Mac's front porch, one hand frozen mid-air, while she gathered the courage to knock. She clutched his pair of gloves in the other. He probably wasn't home. Saturday night and all. He probably had a date. Or something to do other than sit at home. Like her. It's exactly what she'd been doing. *Knock already.* She did so, her breath catching in her throat. Why was this hard?

"I'm not in there."

She spun around, her free hand clutching her chest. "You scared me." She held out the gloves she came to return. "I thought I'd return these. In case you needed them."

"Come in," he said, reaching around her to unlock and open the door.

Left standing on his porch, gloves still clutched in her

hands, she didn't have much choice. She followed suit, closing the door behind her. Stopped to look around, she was surprised. "Nice place, Mac. Not at all what I expected."

He took off his coat, hanging it on a hook inside the door. "Thanks, I think. What did you expect?"

There was a new edge to his voice she had somehow caused. "I don't know. Maybe a man cave?" she joked, attempting to lighten the mood. She glanced around, taking in the overstuffed couch and colors of the mountains. The burgundy and hunter green were masculine but warm.

He searched her face, almost as if trying to read her mind. "Oh. Can I get you a drink? Soda? Juice? Water?"

"Have any scotch?"

A bark of laughter accompanied one raised eyebrow. "With a last name of Mac Gregor? What do you think? How many fingers?"

"Two, please."

"Coming right up." He grabbed a bottle of Glenfiddich and two glasses, carrying them to the couch. "Have a seat."

She stood there for a moment, rooted to the spot. Every fiber of her being screamed for her to leave. But she had been running from life for the past year and a half. She took off her coat and scarf, dropping them over the back of a chair. "I think I will."

Mac poured the alcohol into two glasses, handing one to her. He raised his, murmuring 'Slainte' before taking a sip.

She downed half of hers in a single gulp, more for courage than the taste, and coughed while her eyes watered. "Smooth," she joked.

"Not when you drink it like that."

She took a smaller sip this time, keeping the glass in her hand. "I didn't come to only return your gloves. I, uh, wanted to thank you."

"For what?"

"For giving me the kick in the ass I needed."

"Oh? How?"

"By telling me about Paige and Quinn."

He rubbed the back of his neck. "Uh, I didn't mean to upset you."

She held up one hand to stop him. "Please. You have no reason to apologize. I was lost in my own sadness, I failed to see what was happening right in front of me. You'll be happy to know they will be announcing their date any second."

"Great! I've never seen two people who belong together more than them."

"Agreed." She drained the last of her whisky, setting the glass down.

He did the same before refilling both. The first glass created a pleasant warmth in her belly. "And how do you feel about the wedding?"

"I'm thrilled for them."

"But?"

He had more perception than she gave credit. "But it won't be easy for me. Andrew was the love of my life." She took another sip. "I know people don't understand. We had just met. It happened very fast." She glanced at her left hand, where his ring didn't rest anymore. "It was real."

"Of course, it was. A. J. talked about you all the time."

She saw him glance at her left hand. "Thank you. I took it off. Not long after the funeral. It hurt too much. Mocked me."

He nodded. "I can't imagine."

They fell into a comfortable silence, both sipping their drinks. She thought about Paige and Quinn, right now planning their wedding. And for the first time in too long, she felt joy. They belonged together. And she would be there, celebrating with them. And if her already battered heart broke a little more, she'd deal with it then.

"What's next for you, Amy? Will you go back to teaching?"

She roused herself from her thoughts. "I don't know. Maybe. I miss the little monsters. And having a purpose."

"That's a good sign. Wanting a purpose again."

"I hope so." She raised her empty glass. "Could I get one more, please?"

Mac poured her another, only one finger this time. "How did you know where I live?"

"I asked Paige. Who asked Quinn. Or maybe she already knew. I'm not sure." Things became muddied in her mind. Might be the scotch.

"Paige would have known. She's been here."

"Ah. She did tell me what a nice guy you are."

"Nice? Not exactly the way a man wants to be described." His grimace backed up his words.

"What's wrong with being nice? Would you prefer to be rotten or mean?" She closed her eyes for a moment then the room spun a bit around her. "Maybe I've had enough," she mumbled before falling asleep.

*****

Mac watched the scotch work its magic. Amy's head lay back against the couch. Her last drink sat untouched on the coffee table. He held his, savoring the burn as he took a sip. How had they ended up here?

If someone had told him this morning Amy Windsor would pass out on his couch, he would have laughed. Long and hard. But there she lay, blonde hair down and around her shoulders like a soft cloud. He finished his drink.

He ran a hand through his short, thick hair and thought about the perversities of life. When he'd first heard of her engagement to A.J., Mac couldn't believe it. Thought it must've been a joke. The ice princess, as he had always thought of her, marrying a firefighter? He'd have given anything to see the expression on her brother's face when he heard the news.

But A.J. had loved her with his whole heart. And she him. Before an arsonist took it all away from them. Now, here she was, passed out on *his* couch after drinking *his* scotch. The universe certainly had an odd sense of humor.

She shifted a bit, as though trying to get more comfortable. He sighed and stood up. He couldn't leave her here. Picking her up slowly to avoid waking her, Mac carried her into his spare room and laid her on the bed. He grabbed a blanket from the foot of it, covering her against the winter chill. He stood there, watching her in the dim light from the hallway for a moment before turning away. He didn't want to be that guy.

Chapter Four

Sunlight poured into the bedroom, stabbing Amy's already sensitive eyes. She pulled a pillow over her head to shield them, then froze. This wasn't the heavy, downed pillow she preferred. Where was she? She threw off the pillow and sat up. Much too quickly. Her head pounded, and the room shifted. She glanced down at the unfamiliar blanket and her fully clothed body. Relief poured through her for a moment. Until memories of drinking with Travis Mac Gregor of all people flooded through her addled brain.

A muffled curse reached her ears, followed by the banging of pots or pans. What was he doing? She inched her way upright before noticing a glass of water and bottle of ibuprofen sitting on the nightstand. She shook two into her hand, then added another for good measure before swallowing them. After she gathered her courage, she stepped from the bedroom.

Standing at the edge of the kitchen, she smiled at the sight before her. Mac had eggs going in one pan, bacon in another while he slid bread into the toaster. "Coffee's ready if you are."

"You may have saved my life," she murmured, brushing by him to reach the coffee. "Need some?"

"Already on it," he replied, holding up a mug. "I'm

inhuman until the first jolt hits my brain."

"Good to know." Not that she'd be seeing him first thing in the morning again. "I'm not home."

"Noticed it, did you? Nothing gets by a Windsor." He glanced at her; his piercing green eyes trained on her face.

She turned away when her face heated. "Yes, we Windsors are very observant. What I meant was, how did this happen?" She poured creamer in her coffee, more to busy her hands than anything.

He didn't answer right away. He turned back and she watched him transfer a mountain of fluffy scrambled eggs and some bacon to two plates. He grabbed the toast, distributing it as well, before heading to the table. "Let's eat."

His not answering her question didn't go unnoticed, but she left it alone for the moment. Instead she sat across from him and stared at the impossible amount of food. "Are we expecting company? Maybe a football team?"

One half of his mouth lifted before he shoveled in a forkful of eggs. He chewed and swallowed. "Not to my knowledge." Then his gaze roamed over every visible part of her. "You need to eat."

"I'm not too hungry," she muttered.

"You're thin, Amy. Too thin. Eat something."

Instead of arguing, mostly because he wasn't wrong, she took a bite of eggs. And moaned with her mouth full. "Those are amazing."

"My Grandmother Mac Gregor would be pleased. The cheddar makes all the difference."

"I thought bachelors didn't cook. Andrew couldn't..." She stopped, fork in mid-air.

"Cook? I remember. He hated when his turn to cook for the station came up."

"I'm sorry," she whispered, appetite gone.

"Why? He was a big part of your life. It's normal to talk about him."

"I don't. Not much anyway. It takes too much effort. Makes me sadder."

"I get it. But he was a part of your life. I think you should talk about him, the time you spent together."

She nodded and pushed another bite of eggs into her mouth, swallowing around the lump in her throat. "I'm not much of a cook either. Ask my mother. She tried to teach Paige and me. Andrew and I ordered takeout. A lot."

"Takeout gets old. And I've been on my own a long time. Learning to cook made sense. I had a good start, being raised by my grandmother." He drank some of his orange juice.

"You were? I didn't know."

"Why would you?"

"Excuse me?"

"Why would you know I was mostly raised by my grandmother? At least after my father died."

"Oh. I don't know. Where is your mother?"

His mouth settled into a line resembling granite. "Good question. Don't know. Don't care. She left not long after I was born. Apparently being married to a no-good drunk had lost its appeal by then. She didn't let having a baby stop her."

She remembered the rumors about his father; he drank a lot and was mean to his son. But Mac had been several years older than her, closer in age to her brother, Alex. She hadn't known him in school. "I'm sorry."

"Don't lose sleep over it. It's not like we travel in the same circles."

She set down her fork and waited until he met her gaze. "Doesn't the chip on your shoulder get heavy after a while?"

Fire blazed in his eyes. "Don't fret, princess. I'm strong."

She sat straighter in her chair. "Princess?" Alex would be proud of the Windsor in her voice.

"It's how I've always thought of you. Seems to fit."

"For someone who doesn't know me very well, you seem to have a lot of opinions." She continued to eat, but the once delicious food now tasted like cardboard.

"I know enough."

"What's my middle name?"

He looked up from his plate. "What? How would I

know?"

"Exactly. You don't even know my full name. But it doesn't stop you from thinking you know all about me." She stood before she said something she regretted. "Thank you for breakfast and taking care of me last night. I'll see myself out."

She turned and left the kitchen, searching for her boots and coat. She heard him call her name but didn't slow.

*****

Mac's food grew cold as he sat waiting for his temper to do the same. He had gone one step too far calling her princess to her face. It was bad enough he'd called her that in his head all these years. He'd regretted it the moment the word left his mouth. Until she became a Windsor right before his eyes. The straight back and haughty tone reminded him why he'd dubbed her princess to start. Still, the nickname wasn't fair. She had lost the love of her life and suffered greatly. Having money couldn't protect anyone from pain.

He marched to the sink and threw the remainder of his breakfast down the disposal. He'd lost his appetite. The old, familiar hurt along with reluctant guilt spurred him down to his home gym in the basement. He threw himself into his usual routine, the familiar exercises and effort required numbed the memory of the pain in her eyes.

An hour later and dripping sweat, Mac headed for the shower. He felt the rush that came with knowing he'd pushed his body to the limit. But the remorse lingered. She deserved better than how he'd treated her. And she wasn't wrong. The chip on his shoulder did get heavy. Being born a Windsor, with all it entailed, wasn't her fault. Having parents who didn't drink themselves to death or abandon her didn't make her a princess. It made her a lucky girl. One who had suffered in her own way.

Standing under the hot water, Mac's mind drifted back to the day of A.J.'s funeral. Her family, including Paige, had flanked her, trying to shield her from the awful truth of the day. But nothing they did could help. A.J. was still gone. Amy was still bereft. Being a Windsor hadn't protected her. He leaned his head against the tiled wall, allowing the water to wash away the sweat. But it couldn't touch the regret. He had to apologize to her.

He got out and got dressed, deciding to go find Quinn rather than Amy. He'd let her cool down first. Hopefully, Quinn had good news. He could use some. He left the house in search of his friend.

A few minutes later, he pulled into Quinn's driveway. Paige struggled getting too many grocery bags from the back of her ridiculous car. "Let me help you," he called by way of greeting.

She whirled around. "Oh, thanks, Mac. I hate to make more than one trip. Even when I know I have to."

He took most of the bags from her then followed her to the house. Originally Paige's home, Quinn moved in last year. After A.J. died and Quinn freaked out, breaking things off with her. He came to his senses shortly afterward, begging her forgiveness.

"Have you picked a date?"

"New Year's Eve."

Shock stopped him in his tracks. "This New Year's Eve? As in less than a month away?"

"Yes, this New Year's Eve. Why wait? Especially since Amy has turned a corner." Her face fell. "I didn't mean it."

"It's okay. I know what you meant. I think it's great you put your life on hold to support her." He may not understand it, but he admired it.

She shook her head. "You have it wrong, Mac. She's my sister, for all intents and purposes. I didn't want to do this without her. I knew she'd come to me when she was ready." Her face brightened. "And now she did."

"But you guys put off your wedding for over a year," he protested. He didn't understand.

"Honey, she's family. And family's all that matters."

The thought left him further out in left field. To him,

family meant betrayal and loss. Except his grandmother. "Still, Paige, a whole year."

They had gained the front porch by now. She set her bags on the floor, indicating for him to do the same, before leading him to the swing. "Come sit with me a minute."

She waited until he did as she asked. "Mac, I know you didn't have the Norman Rockwell upbringing."

"Neither did you, really." Paige's parents had died in a car accident when she was twelve. Amy's parents, best friends of the deceased couple, took her in that very day. And no one looked back.

"True. But I had the security of a loving family, even if they weren't my biological one. I remember your grandmother. She was a sweet woman. But she was all you had. Amy means everything to me. And after what happened." She stopped, taking a big breath and exhaling slowly. "Sorry. It still feels unreal sometimes."

He let his own breath out in a rush. "Believe me, I know."

"Of course, you do. After losing A.J., Amy lost herself as well. And my job was to be there for her. Help her. Encourage her. Somedays, bully her into eating. Families do this for each other. They have your back. I could have done all that and still married Quinn, but it wouldn't have felt right." Her smile spread across her pretty face. "And now it does."

"I hope Quinn understands how lucky he is."

"Oh, I do," the man himself answered, coming through the front door.

"I should hope so," replied Paige with a bit of sass in her voice.

Mac got off the swing and crossed to his friend. "Congratulations, by the way. I hear the big day is right around the corner."

"Which brings up a question." Quinn grinned. "Mac, how would you like to be my best man?"

He slapped him on the back in answer. "Well, all right! You know I'd be honored. What do I have to do?"

"Get him to the church on time," joked Paige.

"Got it."

"And plan the bachelor party."

The words earned a scowl from his fiancée. "As long as it doesn't involve naked women."

"Ah, honey, you're no fun."

She threw up her hands. "Fine. Have your naked women. But know it means there will be naked men at the bachelorette party." She burst out laughing at the scowl on Quinn's face.

"Well played, Paige." Mac turned to the groom. "I think you've been bested."

"Not the first time. And I know it's far from the last." He plucked her off the swing and twirled her around while she shrieked.

Mac felt like an intruder. He looked away when Quinn planted a kiss on her mouth. He wanted that. All of it; the laughter, partnership, someone to come home to at the end of the day. But where to find the right woman? He loved Windsor Falls and never wanted to live elsewhere, but he knew everyone. Had dated the decent single women. The curse of the small town reared its ugly head.

He glanced back at Quinn and Paige and cleared his throat. Loudly.

His friend came up for air. "Sorry, not sorry."

Mac picked up most of the grocery bags. "Let me at least take these in for you."

Quinn grabbed the remainder and followed him into the kitchen. "Did you stop by for a reason? Not that I'm not glad to see you, of course."

"Nice recovery," quipped his fiancée.

He shuffled his feet. "No reason."

"Why don't you show him the new shed out back, honey?"

"Uh, okay." Quinn led the way out into the back yard.

Finn, Paige's dog, bounded up to him, greeting him like a long-lost friend. Mac ruffled his silky ears. "Not much of a watchdog."

"Well, he might lick you to death. But we aren't out here

to discuss Finn. What's on your mind?"

Mac grinned back at the house. "Perceptive, isn't she?"

"Yes, and much more."

Mac let out a breath, the chilly air turning it to frost. "Uh, Amy spent the night." He realized his mistake as soon as Quinn's eyebrows met his hairline. "Let me rephrase. Amy came over to return my gloves. Before I knew it, she downed a couple glasses of whisky and passed out on my couch. She slept in my guest room."

"But Amy doesn't like you."

"Gee, thanks."

"Well, you don't like her either."

"It's not that I don't like her."

"Really?"

Mac watched Finn run crazy circles in the remaining snow. "I don't know her. I don't care for what she stands for."

"Meaning?"

"Oh, you know, crazy wealth and everything you ever wanted handed to you on a silver platter." He regretted the words the moment they left his mouth. But he couldn't take them back.

"Which Amy never chose. Not to mention, it sounds like something an insecure teenager would say."

"Tell me again how you're my friend," he muttered.

"You know I am. As you know, for all her privilege, she still suffered a terrible loss. Money doesn't make up for a warm body in bed with you. If you asked her, I bet Amy would give it all away to have A. J. back."

Mac's shoulders slumped. "You're right. It was a foolish thing to say."

"An even more foolish thing to believe. You've never liked the Windsors, but I'm marrying into them. You'll have to get over it."

"I know. I will. But don't count on my becoming buddy, buddy with Alex." Years of resentment burned in his gut at the thought of Amy's older brother.

Quinn threw back his head and laughed. "He's still not

my favorite. Nor am I his. Especially after asking Paige to marry me. But he's coming around."

"Must be your charm."

"Must be. Or maybe it's because Paige loves me, chose me."

"Doesn't hurt."

"Tell me more about Amy spending the night. I'd give anything to have been there this morning. Awkward much?"

"That's one way of putting it." He stared at the bare branches of a tree, remembering how she felt like no more than a feather when he carried her to the guest room.

"What? Think any harder, and you'll start a fire."

"She's not well. I don't mean she's sick or anything. She's, well, not herself."

"I don't imagine she would be. She's broken-hearted. The first few months sucked. Paige barely left her side."

"She's too thin, weighs no more than a feather."

"And you would know this how?"

He couldn't blame the frigid air for the heating of his face. "I, uh, carried her to the guest room."

Quinn said nothing, but his eyebrows rejoining his hairline did the talking for him.

"It's not like that! She passed out on the couch. I couldn't leave her there."

"You're a good man, Mac." Quinn clapped him on the shoulder then whistled for Finn. "I'm about to freeze off something I am very attached to. Let's go inside."

He followed his friend, not really listening to him spout off about wedding plans. He thought about a certain blonde with clear, green eyes.

Chapter Five

The next morning, Amy swung her legs out of bed, toes curling on contact with the icy hardwood floor. *Today is another chance.* These words had become her mantra over the past few weeks. She'd grown impatient and restless with her life. Or lack thereof. Andrew would not have wanted this for her. Yet, every day, she got up, stated her mantra, then failed to live up to it.

But not today. Before doubt and grief could reel her in, Amy threw on winter weight sweats and laced up her sneakers. She grabbed her stuff and dashed out the door. Without even waiting for her car to warm up, she drove to the center of town and parked on a side street. Without stopping to stretch, she set off at a slow jog, fighting for breath in the early morning chill.

Running, much to her friend Paige's chagrin, had always been Amy's choice of exercise. Her way to steady herself, gain focus. In the past, she loved running the quiet streets of Windsor Falls with only the sound of her sneakers hitting the pavement for company. Running on the back roads near her parents' home wasn't as much fun.

Then Andrew died. And everything that ever meant anything to her died with him. She lost her sense of taste and saw no reason to eat. Going out, having fun, without him, became unbearable. So, she didn't. God only knew why Paige had stayed with her, but she was grateful she had.

Fueled by anger at what she'd lost, Amy pushed herself. She pumped her legs, running until her lungs burned for oxygen. And she ran still. Pushed herself until there was nothing left. She collapsed onto a bench on Evergreen Street, Windsor Fall's version of Main Street, USA. She rested her elbows on her knees, lowering her head, and sucked in air. A bottle of water appeared before her eyes. She clutched it in both hands and drank more than half of it.

"Easy now. I'd rather you didn't puke on my new running shoes."

She closed her eyes on Mac's smooth baritone. Of course, it would be him. "I'll keep it in mind." Would there ever be a time when she wasn't putting her foot in her mouth around him? She closed her eyes and held the cool bottle to her neck, concentrating on her breathing. Even though the temperature hovered below freezing, her mad dash left her flushed and overheated. She felt rather than saw him sit beside her on the bench.

"New Year's Eve, huh?"

Amy opened her eyes and turned to look at him. "Doesn't leave much time for planning. But then, my mother is already on it. She's a force to be reckoned with." She took another drink of water. "I owe you a bottle."

"I'll put it on your tab, what with the whisky and breakfast and all."

"Not to mention the night in your guest room." She laughed, the sound rusty and foreign to her own ears.

"Nah. That was my fault for letting you drink too much."

Amy leaned back into the bench. "Do you run every day?" Despite wearing heavy sweats like hers, she could tell he was in good shape.

"Yes, ma'am. On days I'm working, I use the treadmill at work." He laughed at her scrunched-up nose. "Yeah, I don't care for it either."

"There's something about the outdoors. And running. It's

always been my escape. The thing that centers me."

"Beats heroin." He took the bottle from her hands, finishing it in one, long gulp. "Or drinking."

She felt the heat creep across her cheeks. "I promise it was a one off."

"You don't drink?"

She shook her head, long blonde braid whipping. "I do. For fun. But not to forget."

"Because there isn't enough whisky in the world."

She turned her head, staring into his sea green eyes. "Agreed. How about you?" She doubted he did, given his father drank himself to death.

"Oh, I like a local IPA like the rest of the guys I hang out with. But I also know where to draw the line."

As she'd thought. "Smart."

"What with the drunk for a dad and all."

The smile slid from his face. She reached out, placing a hand on his arm. "I didn't know your dad, Mac, but I do know you're not him."

"How? How do you know?" His gaze never left hers.

"Because Paige vouched for you."

"Oh. Just like that?"

"Yes. We're family."

"I see."

She tilted her head, trying to figure out what thoughts swirled through his mind. "I'm not sure you do. Paige and I are sisters in a way different DNA doesn't change. We were there for her in her darkest moment. And she was there for me when-" She stopped because words wouldn't make it past the lump in her throat.

Mac covered her hand with his larger one. "When you needed her."

She nodded at the lack of question in his voice.

He stood, pulling her from the bench with him. "Sitting here in the freezing cold isn't doing your muscles any good. I'm willing to slow my pace a bit." He took off at a moderate pace, tossing a challenge over his shoulder. "See if you can keep up."

Her competitive nature stirred somewhere deep within her. "I'll give it my best shot."

*****

Mac cut his pace, wondering what the hell he was doing. *Running with Amy Windsor.* Who would have guessed it? But for all his dislike of her family, she seemed like a nice person. A nice person who struggled to find her way back after a terrible loss. She earned credit for it if nothing else.

They ran in silence for a mile at a pace his grandmother could do, if she were still alive. He didn't break a sweat, yet her labored breathing sounded at his shoulder. Taking pity, he stopped. "Pathetic, Windsor." He hoped she took his jibe in the spirit he meant it.

"I know," she gasped, and stuck out her tongue at him. "Give me a few weeks to get back to fighting weight."

She straightened and looked at him. The weight of her gaze did something funny to his stomach. "You didn't have to do this."

Mac shifted his weight from one foot to another. "I know."

Her smile, the first genuine one he'd ever seen from her, beamed brighter than the early morning sun. "Thank you."

"No worries. I'm working tomorrow, but I might find myself at the same bench around the same time the day after. If you're up for it."

Her green eyes gleamed like emerald in the sun. "Challenge accepted."

"Good. Consider yourself warned. I won't be running at a snail's pace next time."

"I may be out of shape, but I can hang."

"Brave words. See you then." He turned and started off at his normal pace, forcing himself to not look back at her. Then he set a faster pace, maybe showing off. Just a little. He shook his head at his own stupidity. Showing off for Amy Windsor?

What was the point?

He continued through town and down a side street, staying in the middle where the snow had worn away. He thought he knew her. Had her pegged for all these years. Spoiled princess. Big fish in a small town. Now, he wasn't sure. His Grandma Mac Gregor would have called her an enigma wrapped in a puzzle, misquoting Winston Churchill. She also would have boxed his ears for judging her in the first place. In fairness to Amy, princesses didn't usually become kindergarten teachers. She hadn't exactly been jetting around the world.

And princesses weren't supposed to lose their princes. This new Amy, post A. J. intrigued him. She had spunk, and a sense of humor, but maintained her air of fragility. Like a strong wind might blow her down. Not that he thought about her. He kicked it up a notch, setting a brutal pace. Until his only focus was the air moving in and out of his lungs.

*****

Amy stood there, watching Mac until he ran from sight. Then she turned and headed back to her car, wincing as her long unused muscles protested. She thought about her new running partner and his mercurial moods. One minute he disliked her for her last name and money, the next he offered to run with her. *Men!* A long, slightly bitter laugh escaped her. What did she know about men? Andrew had been her one serious relationship. He'd asked her to marry him short weeks before he died. And she's said yes. Yelled it to the mountain tops.

Before him, she dated of course, but nothing serious. She'd found most men more interested in her name or bank account. Others too intimidated by those or her looks to even try. Neither held any interest for her. She caught her reflection in a passing store front and grimaced. Surely her looks wouldn't intimidate anyone now. But they might frighten them away.

Enough was enough. She whipped out her phone, sending a quick text to her hairdresser. Something had to be done about the unkempt locks. She smiled and set off at a jog. One thing on her impossibly long list could be checked off.

Later, Amy let herself into her childhood home. *Another thing she needed to change.* Paige and her mother had brought her here the day Andrew died. She didn't remember much about the day, just the endless tears and their family doctor sedating her. And she'd never left. At first, the thought of returning to the condo they'd shared crippled her. Then, as time passed, staying in the cocoon of her childhood home became easier. She curled her lip on the thought. The easier path had become her default.

"Amy, is that you?" her mother called from the kitchen.

"Yes, Mama." She dropped her keys and purse on the entry table and followed the delicious scent of her mother's famous chicken and dumplings into the heart of their home. She stopped at the doorway to watch her mother fuss near the stove. How many times over the years had she viewed this scene? Still, a lump formed in her throat. She clung to the familiar, and safe, these days. She rushed in, grabbing her mother in a hug.

"Oh," exclaimed Susan Windsor. She returned the hug before stepping back. Amy stifled a chuckle at her mother's rounded eyes. "Oh, honey! You look amazing."

She touched the ends of her newly salvaged hair. "Miss Hattie Sue gave me 'the look.'"

Her mother chuckled. "I'm sure she did."

"Then she hugged the stuffing out of me and told me to eat." Miss Hattie Sue was a legend in Windsor Falls. No one knew her true age, nor was brave enough to ask. She was as famous for her lack of filter as her excellent styling. But her salon, Hattie's Hair Haven, drew customers of every age, from blue-haired older ladies to Amy and Paige.

Her mother dabbed at her eyes. "Well, you look lovely." She reached out, stroking Amy's once again silky tresses.

The all too familiar lump grew in her throat. "Mom, it's only hair," she commented, knowing it was much more.

Susan grabbed a tissue and shook her head. "No, honey, it's not."

"I know. It's a step, I guess. One of many small ones. I went running this morning, too." She left off the part about Mac joining her. She had no way of knowing how her mother would react to that bit of information.

Her mother clapped her hands. "Wonderful!"

"Then you'll think this next one is a miracle. I'm moving out."

But instead of whatever she had expected, her mother's face crumpled. She slumped into one of the kitchen chairs. "Oh."

Amy took the seat next to her, covering her hands with her own. "Don't you think it's about time?"

She didn't answer; only nodded and cried harder.

"Mom? What's wrong?" She handed her a bit of scrunched up paper towel lying on the table.

She dabbed her eyes and blew her nose before answering. "It's silly really. And I don't want you to think I'm not happy for you. Because I am. Really. But you won't need me anymore."

"Silly Mama. I'm always going to need you."

"I know. And I am being silly. I loved having you back here."

"My house is less than ten minutes away. And I'm not leaving today. But it's past time I go through Andrew's stuff. Don't you think?" Her stomach rolled at the thought. She hadn't set foot in there for eighteen months, since the day he died. The time had long since passed.

Her mother must have sensed the change in her mood. "We'll help you, Amy. You don't have to do it alone."

"I know, Mom. And I appreciate it." She covered a yawn with her hand. "I might take a nap until Dad comes home. Can't wait to tuck into your chicken and dumplings."

Once she was in her room, Amy curled up on the bed,

pulling an old afghan over her. The time to go through Andrew's things was seriously overdue. And still the thought made her stomach cramp. Maybe if she started slowly, a few things at a time. It was her last thought as she drifted off to sleep.

Chapter Six

A few days later, after a challenging run with Mac, Amy peeked into Paige's classroom. She couldn't wait to tell her the good news. She rapped one knuckle lightly on the window, not wanting to wake the sleeping angels. Her friend's face lit with up at the sight of her, so Amy opened the door enough to slip through.

"What brings you here?" she whispered. She followed her question with a hug.

"Don't scream," she warned. "But I spoke with Mrs. Milton, and she's agreed to place me on the substitute list."

Paige's eyes filled with tears as she shrieked, "Oh my goodness!"

"Shush." She glanced around, happy to note only a few small children stirred but did not awaken from their naps.

"Oops. But can you blame me?" She threw her arms around Amy, hugging her while she bounced up and down.

"It's not a big deal."

"You're coming back to life, Amy. Back to us. It is a big deal! This deserves champagne flowing it's such a big deal."

And then the oddest thing happened. Paige's face turned a distinct greenish grey right before she whirled and vomited in the trash can beside her desk. Amy rushed forward, holding back her friend's ponytail. "Are you okay?"

Paige wiped her mouth with a tissue. The color returning to her face relieved Amy. "I am. Or I will be. In about eight months."

"Oh. Oh, my goodness. Are you saying what I think you're saying?"

And then big, fat tears poured down her friend's face. She nodded. "I'm sorry. It's a lot to process."

"What? Sorry?" Amy gasped. "No, Paige, don't be sorry. I'm thrilled for you." And she was. Even if all the air seemed to have left the room.

Paige searched her face. "Are you sure?"

She pasted a huge smile on for Paige. "Of course, I am. I'm a bit surprised."

"Me, too. And you should have seen Quinn's face when I showed him the stick. He almost fainted."

"Big tough guy isn't so tough after all."

"Not to mention the ridiculously overprotective side this news brought out." But the beaming smile belied her words.

One little boy sat up and called to Paige. Amy took the chance to escape. "Well, I'm going to get out of here. But we will celebrate this news."

"Okay. Great." She closed the space between them to hug her.

Amy fled the classroom, hoping the chilly air outside would help her to breathe. She nodded and smiled at the few familiar faces she passed before exiting the building. She jumped in her car and drove a couple miles before pulling over. Her eyes burned but remained dry, as usual. It bothered Paige and her mom that she hadn't cried since Andrew died. Amy didn't think she had any tears left.

Paige was well and truly moving forward with her life. This explained the wedding coming up in less than a month. And she was happy for her. Really, she was. If only the news didn't tear a bit at the fresh scars on her heart. But that was life. No matter what happened, the world turned. Babies were born. People married. And it was a good thing. Except she was stuck.

*****

An empty water bottle bounced off Mac's arm, pulling him from his thoughts. He looked over at his partner's smiling face. "What?"

"Planning on ordering your lunch?

Mac sat up straighter in the passenger seat of their paramedic truck. He blinked a few times and realized they sat in line in a local drive through. "Oh, I'll take my usual."

Trina lowered the window. "May we have a number one with everything and a milk shake and a number nine with a green tea, please?"

He laughed at the look of distaste on his partner's face. "I ordered a salad, Trina, not snails. You might want to try it sometime."

"Uh, no thanks. And for the judgment in your tone, you can buy today." She pulled up to the window and held out her hand toward him.

He placed a twenty in it. "It was my turn anyway."

She laughed and waited for the change. When she had it and their food, Trina pulled to a far corner of the parking lot and shut off the rig. "Are you going to tell me where you went back there?"

Trying to evade the question wouldn't work. His partner knew him too well. Mac took a big bite of his salad and chewed, wondering how best to proceed. "Don't read anything into this, but I was thinking about Amy."

"Tall, gorgeous Amy Windsor, whose family you've hated forever? Why would I read anything into that?" She laughed then took a sip of her shake. "Yummy! And I always thought there was something going on in your head about her."

He glared at her, knowing it wouldn't do any good. "How can you eat only crap and still weigh no more than a feather?"

"Metabolism and good genes, buddy. Nice try, by the way. Now, out with it."

"I like her. And I mean it literally. She's not what I thought."

"You mean she's not the spoiled princess who wears tiaras and gets her nails done daily? Jets off to far flung places on a whim. You finally caught up. Because the Amy Windsor I know teaches kindergarten with her best friend. At least she did."

"Before A.J. died."

"Right. I may joke about my husband and his man colds, but I don't know what I'd do if I lost Manny." She made the sign of the cross before taking a big bite of her burger.

"We've been running together. Well, jogging is a better word for it, since she hasn't run in a long time. She needs to get back in shape."

Trina gasped then coughed until her eyes watered. After a few moments, she could finally speak. "For a minute there, I thought you said you're running with her."

He shifted a bit under her stare. "I did. I am. Well, I have twice." He told her about running into Amy at the beginning of the week and then yesterday.

"You run? Together? Do you talk?" She couldn't keep the laughter out of her voice. He wasn't sure she tried.

"She needs a friend. She's trying to, I don't know, get back to her life. And running is a part of it." He cleared his throat. "We talk about A.J. sometimes."

"Oh. Is this becoming a regular thing now?"

"We will be running again in the morning in case you were wondering." His pulse kicked up at the thought of spending more time with her. Not that he thought of her *that* way. Sure, Amy Windsor possessed a certain beauty. With long, blonde hair and legs forever. He felt a warmth spread across his cheekbones. "It's not a big deal."

"Remember she's still hurting, Mac. Grieving the loss of her fiancé."

"I'm not likely to forget, Trina, as he was one of my best friends." He huffed out a breath. "We're just friends."

"Good. I don't want to see you hurt."

A call coming through the radio stopped him from responding to her ridiculous statement. As if he could ever be interested in a Windsor. "Lunchtime is over, partner." He clicked his seatbelt as she pulled out of the parking lot, lights and sirens going. All thoughts of Amy Windsor fled.

The next morning, Mac jogged in place beside the bench, trying to keep his muscles warmed up. He glanced at his phone, not for the first time. She wasn't coming. *But why?* Unsure what to think, he dashed off a quick text to Quinn, asking for her address. Without question, he answered with it a moment later. Her condo sat only a few blocks from him. It was worth a shot.

He started running, wondering what he was doing. Did she even live there anymore? He remembered Paige saying something once about her living back with her parents. It was too far to run to and not a place he wanted to go anyway. He'd run by the condo, see if she was there. If not, he'd continue his run.

A few minutes later, he stopped outside an old Victorian on Maple street, named for the huge, old trees lining it. He knew the house had been converted into condos, as he helped his friend Paul move in a few months ago. He hadn't known Amy lived here. He checked his phone again for the number. Unit 1, bottom floor. He stepped up on the porch. A woman came out the front door, carrying a baby. He held open the door as she wrangled a stroller and slipped inside after her.

Before he talked himself out of it, Mac knocked on the bright blue door with the number one on it. He waited, shifting his weight from one foot to the other. A minute passed, timed by the beating of his heart. *What was he doing here?* He turned to leave when the door opened.

"Mac? What are you doing here?"

He turned back, releasing a breath he wasn't aware he'd been holding. She stood there, dressed in sweats which hung on her still too thin frame. She looked as though she'd been dressed to run with him.

"I, uh, got worried when you didn't show up. To run?"

"Run? Oh!" She glanced down at her clothes. "Right. It's

Friday at eight." She held open the door wider. "Come in."

He followed her inside, shutting the door behind him. Open moving boxes sat all around him. "If this is a bad time…"

"What? Oh, no. It's fine. I couldn't sleep. I left the house early and came here." She kicked a box with her sneaker. "I haven't been staying here since he died. And I want to." She glanced at him. "I want to move back in. Get back to my life." She swallowed hard and sat on the nearest chair. "But everything here reminds me of him."

He approached her slowly, carefully, like she was a small bird which might take off in fright. "This can't be easy. Can I help?"

Her huge eyes sought his. In their depths he saw hope, maybe gratitude. "Do you have a plan?" A short, harsh laugh ripped from her. "Because my plan was to remove every trace of him. In order to breathe in here. But everywhere I look sits another reminder of him." She picked up a picture frame. In the photo, the happy couple smiled with the sun setting behind them. "Paige took this the night we told my family about our engagement." She traced a finger over the smiling people in it. "Can you see how happy we were?" Her breath grew ragged.

He took the frame from her trembling hands. "I can. He loved you very much, Amy. Talked about you all the time. We all thought he was nuts at first."

"What? Why?"

"Sorry. I didn't mean it like that. He told Quinn he was going to marry you. After your very first date. He loved you already."

The laugh grew harsher. "Maybe he loved me too much. Maybe I did. That's why it was all ripped away from us."

"A.J. died because he was in the wrong place at the wrong time. He died because a greedy business owner decided the insurance payout was worth more than the property. He didn't die because he loved you and wanted to spend his life with you."

She buried her face in her hands. "I know." She sat up and tapped her head. "At least up here."

"Have you spoken with his parents?"

"I did. They came by yesterday to take whatever they wanted to keep. Now, I have to figure out the rest." Her face crumpled. "I have no idea how to start."

"How about socks and underwear?"

A tiny smile flickered across her face. He'd take it. "What?"

"Baby steps. Right? Let's start with something easy. There are things you'll want to keep. Save those decisions for another day. Today, we throw out all his old socks and underwear. You can't donate those."

She stared at him, her face blank, and he hoped he hadn't gone too far. And then the strangest thing happened. She laughed and threw an empty garbage bag at him. He caught it midair as he joined in her laughter.

"Socks and underwear, it is. This way." She turned and walked into what he figured was her bedroom. Their bedroom. He wavered. But he had started this. *'In for a penny. In for a pound.'* His dead grandmother's voice echoed in his head. He followed her.

Mac had never thought about what Amy's bedroom would look like. But if he had, this wouldn't be it. While decorated tastefully in soothing pastel colors, nothing screamed money to him. Several framed photographs of beaches hung on the walls. He stopped in front of the closest to look closer. "Where was this taken?" The water within gleamed a clear aqua, inviting him to take a dip.

She glanced over her shoulder. "Castaway Cay in The Bahamas." She stood next to him and looked at the picture. "Life was easy then."

He turned to glance at her. "Tell me about Castaway Cay."

She met his gaze and smiled. "My parents told Paige and I they would take us anywhere we wanted for our high school graduation."

"Anywhere in the world?" He'd celebrated graduation in his truck with Trinity Peters, his girlfriend at the time.

"The only stipulation being we had to agree on a place. We chose a Disney cruise." She tapped the photo. "This is their private island and my favorite place ever."

"Again, anywhere in the world?"

She grinned. "We wanted to go on a cruise, and this had one huge advantage. It pissed Alex off." The grin spread. "He's such a snob."

Fire burned in his gut at the thought of her older brother. "You know?"

She tilted her head. "How would I not? Everyone knows what a snob Alex is."

"If you look very closely, you can see the tip of the bow of the ship. The bright red spot." She pointed again.

He leaned in closer to peer at the small, red spot. "How do you know that's what it is?"

"Because I took the picture, silly."

"Really?" he glanced around the room. "Did you take all of these?"

A pink color tinged her cheeks. "I did. It's sort of a hobby of mine."

He whistled, long and low. "Hobby? These make me want to dive in the water. Feel the sand under my feet."

"It's just a photograph."

He walked to another wall. "Where was this taken?" He moved to another. "And this?"

"Okay, I get it," she said on a laugh. "I took both of those in Saint Lucia. We went when we graduated from college; our last family vacation. Although Alex didn't come because of work."

"I've been hearing a lot about the island ever since Flynn and Katie eloped there. It looks beautiful."

"It is. Paige and I had a blast." She burst into laughter, the melodical sound drifting through the room. "Sorry," she said, wiping her eyes. "Wow, I haven't laughed like that in forever."

The sound of her laughter had hit him right in the chest, spreading warmth. "Nothing to apologize for. I like to hear you laugh."

She smiled and turned back to the photo. "Me, too. Paige tried to snorkel in Saint Lucia."

"Sounds like it didn't go well."

"Paige is a lot of things but coordinated is not one of them. But she'd tell you herself. Let's say she'll never go pro."

"How about you? Did you like it?"

"I loved it. But then I'd already learned how to dive years before. I thought snorkeling would be easier for her. There's something freeing about it. Floating through another world. You feel light, carefree. Have you ever gone?"

"No," he clipped. "Maybe we should get started on this." He shook open the trash bag in his hands.

He suppressed a wince when her face closed off. "Sure. Of course." She walked to a bureau and opened the top drawer. "This is as good a place as any."

He wanted to say something to bring back her smile. Something to explain his mood. But how could he do so without sounding jealous? Childish? No, he'd never been to an island or gone scuba diving. Another of the endless differences between them.

"If you're busy or have somewhere to be, Mac, I can get this."

"No worries. I'd like to help." And he would. But the lighter feeling had vanished with his mood change. "In fact, I can do this if it'd be easier for you."

"Thanks, but no. I have to deal with it. Even if it is only socks and underwear." She reached in and grabbed a few pair of rolled up socks. "For someone who didn't think twice about leaving a wet towel on the bathroom floor, he sure kept his clothing neat."

Mac barked out a short laugh. "True at the station as well. He kept his gear neat and in good working order. But watch out on cooking day. Quinn described it as a tornado blowing through."

"Yes, I know all about it."

She threw the socks in the opened bag he held, following them with more and more. An hour later, they'd managed to clear out most of his clothing. Small talk about nothing flowed between them, but he missed the laughter from earlier.

He dropped another bag in the to-be-tossed pile. "Do you want me to take the donation items somewhere?"

"No thanks. My mom volunteers at the community shelter. She could give these things to someone in need. I'm keeping a few items."

He noted the small pile of T-shirts she stuffed back in a drawer. She probably slept in them. For some reason, the idea bothered him. He shook his head at his own foolishness. "Are you staying here now?"

"Soon. Maybe." She laughed. "I'm usually better at making decisions. At least I used to be. I am moving back here. I almost sold the place a while ago, but it would have been foolish. Nothing bad happened here. And I love my house. I'm not quite ready to be all on my own again." She ducked her head. "I know it sounds stupid."

"No, not at all. One step at a time, Amy."

"I feel like I've awoken from a coma. I'm trying to catch up. Paige is getting married and having a... Uh, forget what I almost said."

"Having a baby? I already knew. But only because Quinn walked around looking like he'd won the lottery. They're not telling a lot of people since it's early." He brushed a hair from her face. "Does it make you sad?"

"Yes," she blurted before slapping a hand over her mouth. "Please don't tell Paige I said so. It's not that I'm not happy for her, because I truly am."

"Nothing says you can't feel both. Means your human."

"Maybe. At least I'm feeling something. I felt nothing for a long time..."

Before he could talk himself out of it, Mac walked toward her and enfolded her in his arms. He felt her stiffen before she melted into him. He rubbed a hand up and down her back slowly, murmuring to her. He had less than half a foot on her, something unusual for him. He buried his nose in her hair. She smelled of wildflowers and sunshine. And soft female. He broke the hug and stepped away, clearing his throat. "Uh, let me load up these things for the trash." He grabbed several bags at once and left the room.

Chapter Seven

Amy let out a long, shuddering breath and watched him leave the room without so much as a wave or glance. She wrapped her arms around her middle against the sudden chill she felt. *What had happened?* She didn't understand Mac. Not one little bit. The morning had started tough for her, confronted for the first time with all the physical reminders of Andrew. Then Mac had showed up, making her smile and laugh. Making this whole dreaded project easier for her. Then she'd watched his expression close, and she didn't know why. Now this.

Maybe she was being overly sensitive. This wasn't an easy task for her. She sank onto the bed and took a breath. She'd made it through the majority of his clothing and accessories. She glanced at a corner of Andrew's old shirt sticking out from the dresser drawer. Keeping a few might not be healthy, but she wasn't ready to give them up yet. She'd probably torture herself further and sleep in one. She used to do it when he worked overnight, to feel closer to him. But wearing a shirt now wouldn't bring him back. Nothing would.

The front door opening and closing roused her from her thoughts. She turned her head to the opened bedroom door in time to watch Mac walk back in.

"I came back to get the rest of it."

"Did I do something wrong?"

"No. I have some things I have to do." He didn't look at her.

"Are you working tomorrow? I'll be at the bench."

"I'll be there." He picked up the remaining bags for trash. "Gotta go."

"See you tomorrow," she called in the now empty room. Amy sank onto the corner of her bed and looked around. Someone, either her mother or Paige or both, had been in recently. Everything sparkled. Not a speck of dust to be found. She thanked her lucky stars, once again, for having such caring people in her life.

And then she added Mac to the list. Of all people. The few times she'd run into him previously always left her with a vague sense he didn't like her. But he'd been a rock this week, dragging her back into her running routine. He must run faster and further than he did with her.

Which made the way he left a moment ago all the odder. He seemed angry or upset with her. And she had no idea why.

*****

Mac ran back to where he'd left his truck. After driving back to Amy's house, he threw the garbage bags in the back of his truck and drove away, cursing himself the whole time. The last thing Amy needed was some guy hitting on her. The last thing he needed was to develop feelings for a Windsor. They might live in the same small town, but they also lived in different worlds.

He drove to the station, intent on making up for the lack of a run this morning. Dragging the bags from the back of his truck, he threw them in the dumpster behind the station. Then he hit the weight room.

And it hit right back. An hour later, soaked in sweat and knowing he'd be more than a little sore in the morning, he grabbed a towel and mopped his face.

"Training for a marathon I don't know about?" Chief Henry Wells drawled from the doorway.

"No, sir."

The older man walked into the room and sat on a bench close to Mac. "Then it's either money problems or a woman. And you're too careful with money."

Mac barked out a short laugh. "Got it in one." He liked and respected the chief, but he wasn't comfortable discussing his mixed-up feelings for Amy with him. Hell, he wasn't even comfortable thinking about them.

"Thought I recognized the look." He stood and patted Mac on the shoulder. "You also don't look like you're ready to talk about it. You know where I am when you are."

"Thanks, Chief," he called to his retreating back.

Great! Were his feelings, whatever they amounted to, so obvious? He'd have to be more careful around others.

Mac drove home trying to not think about her. He had a few days off. Usually, he'd head out somewhere. He loved to travel. But with the wedding right around the corner, Quinn might need him here. Plus, he'd promised Amy he'd run with her in the morning. *Idiot!*

His phone rang, and Quinn's name flashed on the screen. He answered, "Speak of the devil. Are your ears burning?"

His friend's hardy laugh filled the truck. "No. Should they be?"

"Nah. I was wondering how the wedding plans are coming and if you need me for anything."

"Funny you should ask. I probably wouldn't be as involved, but we don't have a ton of time. And Paige is feeling a bit under the weather. Yes, I could use some help with a few things."

"Morning sickness?"

"Morning, noon, and night as she says. The doctor assured us it's normal for this stage of the pregnancy. Wow, I'm having a baby."

Now it was Mac's turn to laugh. "Did it just dawn on you?"

"No. Yes. I don't know. It's still very new. And we haven't really told anyone. Although I can't vouch for Paige. I have a feeling she may have."

"Well, Amy let it slip to me earlier this morning."

"Amy? Where did you see her?"

He cursed to himself. No need to have Quinn making more of this than it was. "I...uh... helped her get rid of some of A.J.'s stuff." He hoped to gloss over it. No such luck.

"Really?"

"It's not a big deal. Hey, I'm about to hit the shower. Why don't we grab lunch in a little bit? You can tell me what you need help with."

"Great! How about Bob's around noon?"

"That works. See you then."

"And don't think I missed the fact you didn't answer my question." He ended the call on a laugh.

Mac scowled as he pulled into his driveway. He didn't need questions from Quinn, even if he was his best friend. Especially when he didn't have any answers for himself.

*****

Amy knocked on Paige's door as she walked in. Knocking with them amounted to nothing more than a formality. An enthusiastic Finn greeted her by swarming her legs then immediately flopping to his back and exposing his belly for a rub. She ran a hand through his silky fur, laughing. "Not much of a guard dog, are you?"

"Never," Paige muttered, coming out of the first-floor powder room. She sank into an overstuffed loveseat. "Don't mind me. Vomiting thirty-seven times a day is making me crabby."

Amy threw off her coat and sat next to her. "The little person in there is really making you work for this." She rubbed her arm in sympathy. To her astonishment, Paige burst out crying.

"What if I vomit during the wedding?" She collapsed

against Amy, sobbing.

She enfolded her in a hug. "You're not going to vomit. We'll have a chat with your doctor to make sure."

"Promise?"

"Yes, I do." She continued to rub her friend's back. "Now tell me your latest thoughts about this wedding."

Paige sniffed and sat up. She gave Amy a watery smile. "I'm going to wear my mother's dress."

Her throat felt a bit heavy. "That's amazing! I didn't know you had it."

"I didn't know either. Your mom saved it for me all these years. Can you imagine?"

"Well, they were best friends. And you know she considers you her daughter."

A fresh wave of tears poured down her friend's face. "I know," she wailed.

Amy grabbed a tissue and handed it to her. "Blow. It was meant to be a good thing."

"I know. But everything makes me cry." She blew her nose. "I cry at those stupid commercials, where the long-lost adult son sneaks in and wakes everyone by brewing coffee."

"You always cried at those. Can't blame being pregnant."

"True. I'm hopeless." She patted her belly. "At least I can blame hormones for a while."

"I came by to tell you something huge." She stopped and took a big breath. "I started getting rid of Andrew's things today." She tried to swallow the huge lump in her throat. "Not the easiest thing I've ever done."

"Oh honey, why didn't you tell me? I would have helped."

"I know you would. And I still need your help for the rest of it. To be honest, I hadn't planned on doing it today. But I got up this morning preparing to run, and I went there instead." She let out a shaky breath. "It was time."

Paige gripped her hands. "I wish I had been there with you. The thought of your doing it alone breaks my heart. Promise me you'll bring me next time."

"I will. And I wasn't alone. Mac helped."

She stifled a groan as Paige's eyebrows rose and held up a hand. "He's a friend. Well, sort of." She told her about the running pact. "I didn't show up this morning, and he got worried. Showed up at the condo." Then she laughed, remembering his problem solving.

"Share with the class." She reached in her purse and pulled out a sleeve of crackers. "Don't judge. This is the only thing that helps."

"Of course not. Anyway, Mac really helped me. I sort of floundered, not knowing where to start. He blurted out 'socks and underwear'. And he was right. I can't donate those items and don't feel the need to keep them. It made a perfect starting point. We did so well, we kept going. Got rid of a bunch of his old, ratty workout clothes and sneakers. Things like that. Kept a few T-shirts, but I shoved them in a drawer." She clenched Paige's hands. "They still smell like him."

"This can't have been easy for you."

"Not at all. But it's part of the process. Part of getting back to my life. Baby steps. I want to move back in there. It's time. Way past time really. But I can't be surrounded by all of his stuff. Do you understand?"

"Of course! You have to do whatever makes things easier for you. Grief is a personal, subjective journey. When I lost my parents, I couldn't look at anything they owned. It hurt too much. But over time, those things gave me comfort. Like wearing my mom's wedding dress. Your mother gave me the best gift ever."

"Agreed. I really want to keep busy and live alone again. Not that I'm not appreciative of all my parents have done for me. And you even more so."

"Nah. I only did what any best friend would do. I did what you would do."

Amy laughed. "Okay, enough of the mushy stuff. Tell me what you need for this in less than three weeks wedding."

Paige pulled a binder off the coffee table. "I'm glad you asked," she laughed.

Several hours later, Amy let herself into her parents' home. A note on the fridge told her they were meeting friends for dinner at the club and her dinner only needed warming up. She pulled out a plastic container with her mother's amazing beef stew and slid it into the microwave. She poured herself a glass of wine while she waited.

Paige and Quinn planned a small wedding. Still, the amount of details needing attention boggled her mind. Luckily, her mother lived for this kind of thing. Susan had already booked a small room at The Mountainside Lodge, where their good friend Kat De Luca happened to be the head pastry chef. Now, they could cross the cake off the list. And Paige had her mother's dress, so other than alterations and cleaning, she was set. She'd left Amy's dress up to her. Quinn had enlisted Mac to help him with things like music, their tuxedos, and finding an officiant. Both the ceremony and reception would take place at The Lodge.

The dinging of the timer dragged her back. The amazing aroma also helped. Running had brought back her appetite. She sat at the kitchen table with her stew and wine and thought about the upcoming wedding as she ate. Amy doodled some thoughts and ideas. She waited for the stab of pain and regret, but it didn't come. She would have been married over a year now, if Andrew hadn't died. But he had. And she was still here. With family and friends who loved her. And then a thought came to her for the first time in over eighteen months. She was lucky.

Chapter Eight

Her breath crystalized in front of her as Amy warmed up. She jogged in place next to their meeting bench, half wondering if he would show. Running with Mac had grown important to her in the past week. Not that she'd be sharing the knowledge with him. Still, she hoped he made it today.

"I hope you stretched first," he commented, rounding the corner near her. He slowed to a walk, stretching his arms out over his head.

"Yes, sir, I did," she answered with a snappy salute.

"Very funny. I won't be letting you off easy today." He took off at a staggering pace.

"Hey," she called to him. "That's not fair." Never one to lose a contest, Amy kicked it into high gear. She caught him within a block, knowing he let her.

"Not bad for your first week."

Except the part where her lungs burned. "Sure," she wheezed at him. "Wait until I'm back in form." If this didn't kill her first. She kept the thought to herself. She fell into step with him, running more easily than a few days ago.

"I've missed this."

"Running is therapy for me. And not just physically. We see a lot of shit at work. This helps me to clear my head."

"I can only imagine. I don't know how you do what you

do." They stopped at a red light, jogging in place. "One day, I'll ask you about *that* day. Not today, though." She took off at the green light.

"I'm here when you're ready."

They continued on, getting in a little over three miles. The last one hurt, but she stuck to it. Windsors never admitted defeat. Mac halted in front of Breakfast Haven, a small restaurant catering to breakfast and lately lunch. He tilted his head toward it. "Care to buy me breakfast?"

She laughed at him but agreed, noting he held the door for her. If nothing else, he was a gentleman. "Ooh," she cried at the rush of warm air greeting her. She pulled off her gloves and band covering her ears. "It feels heavenly in here. What will you have?"

His green eyes widened. "You know I was kidding, right?"

"You can buy next time. Does it bother you to let a woman pay?"

"Hey, if a beautiful woman wants to buy me breakfast, I'm all for it!"

She stood there in her too big running clothes, straggly braid and not a lick of makeup. *And he thinks I'm beautiful?* It didn't matter. She'd had her shot at happiness.

A waitress led them to a booth. "Can you order a hot chocolate and bagel with cream cheese for me?" She didn't give him time to answer, fleeing for the restroom.

*****

Mac watched her go, wondering what had happened. He gave the waitress their order before sliding into the booth. He thanked the waitress when she brought his coffee and played with the spoon while it cooled. He didn't understand women, never had. Amy seemed even more mysterious to him. He understood she'd suffered an enormous loss. Maybe this was how she dealt with it.

When he was about to go check on her, she rejoined him,

flashing an overly bright smile at him. "Sorry."

"No need to apologize. Are you okay? I got worried."

"Yes." Her smile dimmed. "Maybe. Who knows?"

He sat back in the booth, giving her the time he believed she needed, and watched her shred her napkin into a paper blizzard.

"I seem to have lost my people skills somewhere along the way," she offered by way of explanation.

"Oh. It's only me. I know we don't know each other very well, but maybe it could make this easier."

She cocked her head at him. "How so?"

"We don't have any history, therefore no expectations. We're new friends. No pressure."

"I can do that."

The waitress returned, dropping off Amy's drink and their food. He waited until she smeared cream cheese on her bagel. "One ground rule. We don't lie to each other. Ever."

She froze, mid smear. "Why would I lie to you? I don't make it a practice to lie to anyone."

"Good. Then tell me what I did to upset you when we got here." He took a bite of his fried egg sandwich and waited for her answer. He didn't have to wait long.

"You implied I'm beautiful," she blurted, dull red creeping across her cheekbones.

"But you are beautiful, Amy. I imagine you already know." He watched in disbelief as she squirmed in her seat.

"No one has told me since Andrew died," she whispered. "And I don't need any complications in my life, Mac. I need friends."

And the lightbulb flicked on in his mind. "Oh, you think I was asking you out?"

"Uh, no, of course not."

He leaned across the table, crowding her a bit. "I'm not the most subtle of men. If I ask you out, you'll know it." Her widened gaze drew him in. He sat back and picked up his fork. Neither of them needed *that* kind of complication.

"Good to know." She resumed eating while a thick silence

hung over the table.

After a few minutes, he couldn't take it. "Look, I'm sorry. It really was an off-handed comment. Obviously, you're a beautiful woman. But I can appreciate what you've been through and how hard you're working to get back to normal. The last thing I want is to make things harder for you."

"Thank you," she murmured. "I don't know if I'll ever try dating again. I sucked at it until Andrew came along."

"I find that hard to believe. You're stunning. And rich." If the last had a bit of an edge, he couldn't help it.

"And therein lies the hitch. I have good genes behind me. But many men are put off by my looks. Somehow, I'm unapproachable. As for money, having it creates more problems than you'd believe. How do I know when someone likes me for me as opposed to my bank account or name?"

"Has it happened?"

"More times than I care to remember. Being a Windsor in Windsor Falls isn't all it's cracked up to be. Alex is the only one who enjoys it. Andrew never cared."

"I bet he did when he had to meet your family. It couldn't have been easy for him."

"Meaning?"

"He was a firefighter, not a trust fund baby. I'm sure Alex loved that."

"What is your issue with my brother?"

"Alex is a snob. He's quick to make sure everyone in the room knows who he is. And how much money he has. Those are the issues I have with him."

"Have you had a conversation with him since high school?"

"No, and I don't need to or plan to."

"High school was like a lifetime ago, Mac. Aren't you being a little silly?"

"Your brother made my life Hell."

"And we're back." She wiped her mouth on the paper napkin and stood. "You have a huge problem with others having money. Well guess what. It's your problem." She took a twenty from her phone case and threw it on the table. "See what my evil money buys? Breakfast. Have you ever thought, Mac, for even a second that you're the snob?" Her long braid whipped around as she stormed out.

The waitress came by to top off his coffee. "What'd you do to piss her off?"

"I have that effect on beautiful women," he joked. His hands curled into fists, and he felt like punching something. Trying to be friends with Amy Windsor was a mistake.

*****

Amy started running as soon as she left the coffee shop. She ran until the stitch in her side felt like a hot poker. Only then did she slow to a walk. But even walking took more oxygen than she had. She stopped and pulled out her phone. She called Paige, but it went right to voicemail.

"Who does that arrogant prick of a man think he is? Snob? I'm a snob? How dare he!" She stopped, sucking in some much-needed air. "As if I care one whit what he thinks of me and my family. Good riddance. Call me when you get this. I'll be home. Unless I'm in jail for killing the jerk." She ended the call and let her indignation carry her the rest of the way to her car.

What was it with him? Alex could be a jerk, especially back in high school. Although he was older than her and Paige, and they hadn't gone through together. But she knew his reputation. He'd mellowed with time, but he remained the only one impressed with being a Windsor. She preferred people to judge her on her own merits. Still, Mac had no right talking about Alex that way. She couldn't help feeling as though he lumped her together with her brother.

Fatigue washed over her as she pulled into her parents' driveway. The anger had receded, leaving her weary. She slumped back against the seat and closed her eyes for a moment to gather herself. And screamed at a knock on her window.

"Alex, not funny!" she scolded, climbing out of the car.

He smirked. "It was from my view. Why are you sleeping in your car?"

"I wasn't asleep. I was fuming."

"Who has your panties in a twist?"

She laughed. "That doesn't seem like something a snob would say."

"Did you call me a snob?" He followed her into the house. "I'm proud of being a Windsor. How does it make me a snob?"

She glanced up and down at his perfect, not a wrinkle in sight clothing. "How do you stay perfect all the time?"

"Years of practice," he joked. "But seriously, who called me a snob?"

"Travis Mac Gregor if you must know." She kicked off her sneakers and tossed them into the hall closet.

"The paramedic? Should I even care what he thinks?" His tone told her exactly what he thought of Mac and his career choice.

"Gee, I can't imagine why he'd think it. Could you put any more condescension you're your tone?"

"Why should I care what he thinks of me?"

"You shouldn't. You're missing the point."

"Then what is it?"

"Nothing, Alex. This doesn't concern you." She walked into the kitchen and kissed her mother on the cheek.

Susan grinned at her daughter. "I love it."

"Don't you mean you love me?"

"Well, of course. But I love the sound of your bickering." She laughed. "Who thought I'd ever say that?"

And her meaning dawned on her. "I'm sorry, Mom. For making y'all walk on eggshells around me for so long. For everything really."

"Pish! You didn't make us do anything, and I'm happy to see glimpses of your old self coming through."

She snagged a carrot from the pile her mother cut. "Me, too."

"What were you and your brother quarreling over?"

"His being a snob."

"Oh, that."

"I heard you," her brother called from the living room.

"I wasn't whispering. We all know you have your moments, Alex. And we still love you." She turned to Amy. "How did this come up?"

Amy snagged another carrot and sat at the table. "Mac has an issue with our family."

"Quinn's friend? He seems nice enough. He certainly helped Paige when she fainted on the town green."

Amy let out a big breath. "He is nice. In fact, he's helping me get back into running. And sorting through Andrew's things." She waited for the inevitable questions.

The knife slowed. Her mother tilted her head. "Why does he have a problem with our family?"

It wasn't the question she expected. "Apparently, Alex wasn't very nice to him in high school."

"Which was a really long time ago."

"Right? But Mac had a much different childhood than Alex and me."

Susan nodded and reached for an onion. "His grandmother impressed me the way she stepped in and raised him. Now his father was a different kettle of fish. The man cared more for the drink than his only child."

"How do you know?"

"This is a small town, honey. And Windsor Falls comes with the good and bad. The bad being everyone knows a lot about each other. Things got worst after his mother left. Travis must have been only a toddler. Can't have been easy."

"Agreed. But it doesn't mean he gets to judge us. He actually calls me 'princess'?"

To her shock, her mother put down her knife and started laughing. A lot.

"Mom! It's not funny."

"You're right. But it is a little funny." She reached out and stroked Amy's hair. "What's the real issue here? What he called you? Or who called you it?"

"What? I barely know him, Mom."

"Exactly." She handed her daughter a peeler and pointed at the bowl of potatoes. "I love Windsor Falls. Wouldn't live anywhere else. But marrying into the founding family wasn't exactly a piece of cake. Your father's grandparents acted like he chose a serial killer."

Amy picked up a potato and started peeling. "They didn't approve of you? Are you kidding me?"

"They sent your father off to the best boarding school and then an Ivy League college. He was meant to meet the 'right kind' of girl, not some local one. It's why he insisted on public schools for you guys."

"Much to Alex's chagrin."

"Right. Sometimes I swear he's his great grandfather reincarnated. And then there's everyone in the town, thinking they know who and what you are because of your last name."

"Exactly!" A long peel flew when she used more force than necessary. "Mac thinks he knows *me* based on my last name. And who my brother is."

"And you've never cared before him. Interesting."

Amy jumped up and paced the kitchen, waving the peeler. "It's not like that. I don't give a hoot what Travis Mac Gregor thinks."

"Despite all evidence to the contrary. It's okay to care about him, honey. And his opinion, even if it isn't based in reality."

Her heart bounded in her chest like a terrified rabbit. "Mother!" She sat back in the chair. "I just lost Andrew," she whispered.

Susan put down the knife and wiped her hands on a towel. "No, Amy, you didn't. Andrew died eighteen months ago. You're a young, beautiful, single woman. Don't forget it."

"But I don't want to be single." She hung her head. "I miss Andrew."

"Of course, you do. But missing him, shutting yourself off from the world, will not bring him back. You know I'm right."

She raised her eyes to her mother's. "When will I be able to think of him, remember him, without it hurting so much?" She flattened one hand against her chest. "Will there ever be a day when I don't feel guilty about laughing or feeling joy?"

"Everyone grieves differently, dear. Remember when Paige lost her parents? She slept with the light on in her room for over a year. Everything scared her. She wouldn't let us out of her sight for fear something would happen. But she found ways to cope. To move on."

"What if I don't want to move on?"

"I think you've already made the choice to do so. In baby steps." She reached out and wound a chunk of her blonde hair around a finger. "It's like you've awoken from a long nap."

"Or nightmare," she grimaced. "Sometimes it feels like I'm still in it. Sometimes, Mama, I forget. For just a moment. I wake up, excited to start a new day, and then I remember. He's not here. He never will be again. When will it stop?"

Susan gathered her daughter in her arms. "I wish I knew, baby girl. I wish I could take away all the pain for you. I'm not sure it ever stops. Not completely. Maybe it happens less often?"

"In the beginning, I slept wrapped around his pillow, pretending on some level it was Andrew." She squeezed her eyes shut. "In the beginning, I couldn't breathe right. It hurt to take a whole breath. And my heart ached. A physical pain for him. And then it got easier. A tiny bit each day."

"And it hurt you. Because you thought you didn't love him or miss him as much anymore."

"How did you know?"

"I didn't. I guessed because I know you." She kissed her head. "And how does Mac fit into this?"

"He doesn't. Well, he's my friend, sort of. He's Quinn's friend. And Quinn of course is marrying my best friend. I can't escape him." She shook her head. "No, that's not right either. I don't want to escape him. He's been very sweet, helping me through this."

"But? It sounds like there's a but in there."

"He held me in his arms. And it felt good to be held again. Even if he isn't Andrew. And he called me beautiful. He can't go around doing that!"

Susan stifled a laugh. "How dare he? Pitchforks at sunrise!"

"You know what I mean. He can't have any feelings for me. He has to be my friend."

"And you can't have any feelings for him, right?"

"Right."

"And how's it working out for you?"

Chapter Nine

She didn't have an answer for her mother's question. Not even after locking herself in her room to ponder it. Mac couldn't be more than a friend to her. She couldn't have any feelings for him. He was brash and rude to her at times. He spoke his mind without thought of how his opinion might be received. He was not Andrew. And yet, here she was, an hour later, still thinking about it. *What was wrong with her?*

Well, she hadn't had sex in eighteen months. It had to be the reason. Hell, she hadn't even been touched by another man until Mac held her in his arms. Like her mother pointed out. She was young and still alive. She couldn't help feeling something when he touched her. It didn't have to mean anything. Did it?

She needed Paige. Glancing at her phone, she cursed at the time. Still a few hours until her friend finished for the day. She sent off a brief text asking Paige to have dinner with her. She'd calm her down. Set her straight. But for now, maybe a nap. She curled up on her bed, pulling the quilt her grandmother had made over her. Her eyes drifted shut as soon as her head hit the pillow.

"Amy, everything will be okay."

She turned to find Andrew smiling at her in the kitchen of their condo. Her heart swelled at the sight of him. She could smell the sweat on his skin. See the humor in his bright eyes. "I've missed you so much," *she whispered to him.*

"I'm always with you, Amy. Can't you feel me near you?"

"It's not enough, Andrew. I want you to come back to me."

He smiled then. A sad smile that broke her heart. "I know I promised you I would always come back to you. I never meant to break the promise, honey."

"I know. You would never have left me if you had a choice. But, Andrew, I don't want a life without you. I miss you. Sometimes, I miss you so much I can't take a breath."

He moved closer to her, drifted really, and held his hands out to her. "I'll always be with you. In your heart. But it's time to get back to your life, Amy. You deserve to be happy. I want that for you. I always have."

Her throat grew tight as she watched him fade. She reached for him, only to have him dissolve like smoke. "Andrew, stay with me."

She jerked awake, her heart beating in her throat. Throwing off the quilt, she whipped her head around searching for him, his name on her lips. But he wasn't real. Wasn't there. Would never be again. Her shoulders slumped as the reality hit her once again.

Her phone rang, a snappy Christmas tune which meant Paige, who loved the holiday. She snatched it up. "Hey."

"Hey, yourself. Are you okay?"

She winced at the worry in her friend's voice. Hated causing it. "I'm hanging in there. How's your day going?"

"Oh, the usual. Brandon and Timmy got into a fight over who could sit next to Savanna during story time. It starts young."

"Sounds nice. I could use some normal stuff in my life about now."

"I got your voicemail. And text. Dinner sounds great."

Amy didn't answer right away. She regretted the impulsive, ranting message she'd left earlier. "In my defense, Mac can be very annoying." And now she sounded like a child. *Shut up, Amy.*

"Really? He's more like the older brother I never had.

Well, other than Alex."

The thought made Amy laugh. "Good Lord, those two are polar opposites." Either would die at the comparison. "Where and when for dinner? Your choice."

"How about Sadie's at six?"

"Perfect! See you then." Sadie's was a local place, on the order of a slightly upscale diner. The menu boasted home cooking and lots of it. There would be carbs aplenty. Exactly what she needed these days.

A few minutes before six, Amy welcomed the warmth enveloping her as she walked into Sadie's. Several people turned and waved at her before whispering to their companions. She sighed. Welcome to life in a small town. Especially when you happened to be a member of the founding family. She shrugged it off. Most people meant well. Cared about what had happened to her. You took the good with the bad.

A hand waved at her from a booth in the back. Paige had beaten her here. Shocking. She made her way through the crowded space, murmuring hello to various groups of people. By the time she took off her coat and sank into the booth, she felt as though she'd run a marathon.

"Working the crowd, I see," Paige joked.

"The shock value will wear off."

Her best friend leaned in across the table. "People care about you. You know that, right?"

"I do. Still, I'll be glad when it's over." She squeezed her hand. "You look great! Is this the pregnancy bloom I've heard about?"

"This is the I haven't vomited in over twenty-four hours look. Morning sickness is a misnomer. I have morning, noon, and night sickness."

"It's still early days, though. Maybe it will fade as you progress." She mentally patted herself on the back for talking about this without feeling the need to curl up in a ball somewhere.

Paige held up both hands with fingers crossed. "Here's hoping. I have my first obstetrics appointment soon. Until then, I've been reading."

Amy tilted back her head and laughed. "Let me guess. You went and bought every book you could find on the subject."

"In my defense, I've never been pregnant before and have no idea what to expect."

The waitress came and took their orders, promising to return with bread and their drinks in a 'flash.' Paige shook her head. "Is it me, or are they getting younger?"

"Well, it's not us getting older. She didn't look old enough to be working here though. Probably in high school." Although she was only in her late twenties, most days Amy felt much older.

"True, but we look good. Now, you've stalled long enough. What happened with Mac? This time."

She shifted in her seat, not sure where to start without seeming silly. "He told me I'm beautiful. And then he hugged me." She glanced down at her hands, clenched in her lap.

"And no one has done this since A.J. died."

Amy took comfort in the lack of a question mark in her friend's voice. "And that's why I love you. You get me." She smiled at Paige, thankful as always for her never ending support.

"You had a life planned with A.J. A life which included getting married and having a family. And all of it was ripped away from you in the blink of an eye. Since that day, Amy, you've been wrapped in a fog of sorts. Here, but not really. It can't be easy."

You're right about the fog for sure. Having him hug me, feeling his arms around me, brought back what I loved about being with A.J. The connection with another person. Made me realize how much I missed it." She sat back and took a breath. "But it comes at a high price. Not one I'm sure I can pay again."

"You're right. I love Quinn with all my heart." She placed

a hand on her still flat stomach. "And this little person, who I've never met and is the size of a pea. I've already fallen head over heels in love with them as well. And I can't imagine my life without Quinn. Can't imagine the pain of losing him like you lost A.J. But what's the alternative? Never caring? Never loving? Can't live like that either. I roll the dice, love him every day, and hope for the best."

"Understood. And I am happy for you and Quinn. And thrilled for the little person coming next year. But I am not sure I could ever risk my heart again."

"I get it. Really, I do. How did you leave things with Mac?"

"I didn't. I left him sitting in the booth all alone." She paused as the waitress brought them drinks and a breadbasket. She thanked her and grabbed a warm roll. After lathering it in butter, she took a huge bite. And closed her eyes on the explosion of flavors on her tongue, moaning aloud.

"You had a culinary orgasm."

Amy opened her eyes and grinned at Paige. "You may be right. Everything tastes good again."

A huge smile lit her friend's beautiful face. "Warms my heart to see. Now, back to Mac."

"This isn't about Mac, specifically."

Her raised eyebrows spoke for Paige.

"Not really. It's about feeling anything at all again. Taking a chance. Getting back out there."

"And Mac has absolutely nothing to do with it? At all?"

"Well, sure, he got me thinking about it. But it could have been anyone."

"You don't feel anything at all for him. For Mac?"

She took another bite of bread, more to give her time than anything. "He's handsome, I guess. If you go for the big, brawny look."

"Kind of like saying the Mona Lisa is a nice painting. He's gorgeous, Amy."

"Does Quinn know this?"

"Very funny. Quinn, and everyone else, knows there's

only one guy for me. But, I'm not blind. Mac is nice to look at. And loyal. And a great friend."

She threw up her hands. "All right, you win. Yes, he's not bad looking. And he's been very kind to me, helping me with Andrew's things. But…"

"But, nothing. He cares about you, Amy. Why else would he be helping you and running with you in the mornings?"

"But this, and it's important, he thinks I'm a snob because I'm a Windsor in Windsor Falls. He can't see past it."

"He'll get over it when he gets to know you better, Amy. Mac had a very different childhood than we did."

"I know, and I'm sorry for him. But it wasn't my fault. I didn't make his mother abandon him nor his father drink too much. And every time I think we're past it all, he brings it up again."

"I can see how it would be bothersome. Still, I have a hard time imagining it. He's lovely to me."

"Helps being his friend's fiancée."

"True. What are you going to do?"

Their waitress appeared with their food, Salisbury steak for Paige and fried chicken for her. At least she got a slight reprieve, since she had no idea how to answer. She picked up a drumstick and took a bite. The buttermilk coating probably held a thousand calories, but each one would be worth it.

"I'm about to dive into his meal, but you're not off the hook."

She smiled around the drumstick. "Perish the thought. You're a Pitbull when you sink your teeth into something." She swallowed and put down the chicken, wiping her hands on a napkin. "I have to apologize to him for freaking out when he complimented me. You're right, Amy. He is a very nice man. And I look forward to our running sessions. Besides, as you said, he is Quinn's best friend. It's not like either of us is going anywhere."

"No, you're not. And you do have to walk down the aisle together."

The thought sent a cascade of shivers throughout her. "I

still need a dress."

"Yes, you do. I'm sure nothing you own fits you anymore."

"And you'd be right. Besides, I want something new for your wedding. Tell me you're making the guys wear black tie."

"I am, despite all the grumbling. I told Quinn it wouldn't kill him to wear a tuxedo for one night."

"I'm sure Mac feels the same. I've only ever seen him in running clothes and other casual things."

"Oh, I got an earful from him as well. I pulled the bride card. As in I'm the bride, and I say so."

"You go girl! Use it while you can. I'm sure he loved that." An image of Mac dressed in formal attire popped into her mind. It wasn't unpleasant.

"He groaned and complained but saw the light as Quinn did. They make such a big deal out of it. It's only a few hours. And they don't have to get all gussied up like we do, with hair and make-up."

"Or wear ridiculously high heels. Although, at least walking with Mac, I'll be able to." Just shy of six feet herself, most guys didn't appreciate having her tower over them in heels.

"See, there's another of his many redeeming qualities. He's taller than you," Paige crowed.

"Nothing like stating the obvious," Amy grumbled in return.

They finished their meals, discussing possibilities for Amy's dress. They made plans to go shopping over the weekend.

"This will give me a chance to pick up something to wear for the medical center charity ball as well."

"Oh, I forgot. I'll need another dress," exclaimed Amy.

"Are you planning on going?"

"I hadn't thought about it, but now that you mention it, yes." The annual fundraiser supported the local hospital, raising money for different programs. She'd missed last year, but her mother sat on the committee, and she'd always attended before. "Maybe I'll ask my mom if they need any more help. It would give me something to do."

"What a great idea. I'm sure she'd be thrilled to put you to work. You know how crazy she gets as it grows closer. Having my wedding a few weeks prior doesn't help."

"You know she's thrilled about the wedding. Are they having the charity auction again?"

Paige laughed. "Now you know why Quinn agreed to a New Year's Eve wedding. He won't be a bachelor come January."

"He would have agreed to getting married at the courthouse any day of the week. The man loves you."

A rosy glow colored her friend's face. "I know. I'm a lucky girl. But missing being 'sold' for charity is icing on the cake for him."

"We've lost quite a few bachelors recently. I wonder if Mom has had to recruit others."

"Funny you should ask. She grabbed Mac for it a few weeks ago."

Amy had taken a drink of her water and almost spit it across the table at the mention of him. "Really?" she coughed. "How'd she convince him?"

"Have you ever known anyone to say no to your mother?"

"Good point. Still, I have a hard time picturing him being auctioned off. Even for a good cause."

"I'm wondering if he'll wear formal wear or his uniform. Either way, he can't go wrong."

A chill enveloped her, and she felt the room grow silent. The last thing she needed or wanted was a room full of dress uniforms. She heard Paige's voice as though it came from miles away. Andrew's funeral had been filled with fellow firefighters, all wearing their dress uniforms. Despite the ungodly heat of the July day. She stood with his parents as wave after wave of them approached, offering their condolences, until she'd actually wished to black out. If only to escape.

"Amy? Amy? Are you okay?"

She snapped back to the reality of the dinner rush din at Sadie's. She nodded. "Yes, thank you. I may have drifted for a moment."

"I'm sorry," she gushed, enfolding her own icy hands with her warmer ones. "I didn't think. I'm sure dress uniforms aren't a pleasant memory for you."

That was putting it lightly. "No, not so much. Welcome to my life. Things are going to bring the sadness back to me, no matter how much I don't want them to. I have to learn to deal with it." She drank a big gulp of water and gave her a shaky smile.

*****

The next morning, Amy jogged in place to stay warm as she waited for Mac to show. She glanced at her phone. Eight fifteen already. Maybe he had to work. They hadn't discussed his schedule. Shrugging, she took off at a quick clip. Already, her love of running returned to her. Each day she felt a little better, more limber and less winded. It had to count for something.

The first two miles flew by, and she slowed her pace a bit. She thought about the upcoming wedding. She'd be fine. She had to be. Paige needed her to be. First, she needed a dress. Given the wedding would be on New Year's Eve, she wanted a color to suit. Maybe silver or black.

"One day without me, and you're down to a jog?"

The unexpected voice threw her, causing her to break stride and stumble. Two large hands, ones she'd come to recognize, reached out to steady her.

"Don't do that!" she admonished, taking a large gulp of air to slow her racing heart. "You startled me."

"I'm sorry," he said in a tone which made him a liar.

She turned to face him, ready to give him a tongue lashing. But the rising sun set fire to his hair. His smile reached all the way to his eyes, and she let it go. "I didn't think you were coming."

"Sorry for being late. And for yesterday."

It was her turn to smile. The admission cost him. But she wasn't ready to let it go. "This thing you have with my family and money. You have to lose it or else we can't be friends."

He took a step closer, filling her vision. "Is that what we are? Friends?"

"I'd like to think we are." If she hadn't been looking at his face, she might have missed the fleeting change in expression, the slightest dimming of his smile.

"Well, as your *friend*, your pace won't get you anywhere."

"In my defense, I ran the first two miles at a much faster one."

He grinned. "Sure, you did."

"I know the truth. It's all that matters." She stuck out her tongue at him and took off running.

"Hey!" he yelled.

The sound of his sneakers hitting the pavement spurred her on. Of course, he caught her in less than half a block, but she held her own without wheezing. The two ran in a companionable silence for a while until he stopped near the town gazebo.

"What's the matter, old man, have to stop?"

"Old man?" he asked, one eyebrow meeting his hairline. "How old do you think I am?"

"Older than me."

"Well, you are a puppy."

"Some days, I feel like an old dog." She grinned at him. "But not today. And I believe it's your turn to buy breakfast." She took off across the street and headed for De Luca's Bakery. Her friend Kat's bakery offered the most delicious pastry in Windsor Falls.

He passed her and held open the door. "After you."

The competing scents of cinnamon and dough teased her nose. The warmth inside delighted her. She removed her gloves.

"Amy!" shouted Mr. De Luca, coming around the counter to enfold her in his arms. "What a delightful surprise."

She stepped back when he released her and looked him up and down. "You've lost weight, Mr. De Luca. You look fabulous!"

"Thank you, my dear. Ekaterina is like a Nazi about my diet. But, if it gets me more years, then so be it." He looked over her shoulder, a grin lighting up his face. "And you, my friend, my savior. Come in, come in."

She turned to watch the older man envelope Mac in a bear hug, slapping him on the back. The sound reverberated through the nearly empty bakery.

"Mr. De Luca, it's great to see you again. And in much better shape, I might add."

"Yes, yes." He turned to Amy. "This man eats for free. He is one of my saviors from that black day."

The red tinge across Mac's cheekbones amused her. She knew all about the curse of fair skin. "Do tell."

He ducked his head for a moment before relating the details of what had happened. "I was only of doing my job. You got lucky having the doc here."

"You are too modest, my friend. Although having Ekaterina's Sebastian here certainly helped, I would have been a goner without you."

"A win is a win, and you got one, sir. Not everyone does."

"Agreed. Now, what can I get for this lovely couple?"

Amy squirmed but didn't correct him. She had known the bakery owner her whole life. He'd believe what he wanted. "I'll have your biggest cinnamon bun, please."

Mac grinned at her. "Make it two."

The older man waved them toward a table. "Sit, sit. I will bring them to you."

They moved to a table, Mac pulling out her chair first. You had to love Southern men.

"I notice you didn't correct him," he whispered to her, taking off his gloves and hat.

"I've known him too long. He believes what he wants."

"Well, it can only help my reputation, to be seen with such a younger woman on my arm."

She groaned and held up her hands in mock surrender. "Okay, enough already. I'm sorry I called you an old man. You're not old. Just older." She laughed at her own joke.

"Ha, very funny. How old are you anyway?"

"And here I was thinking you were a well-trained Southern gentleman. You never ask a lady her age."

"You're right. Grandma Mac Gregor would skin me alive if she was here."

Mr. De Luca approached their table and set two plates down, each holding the largest cinnamon rolls she'd ever seen." Her stomach gurgled in appreciation.

"Wow! I'll never be able to finish this. But I'm certainly going to try." She broke off a piece and popped it in her mouth. "Oh my," she murmured at the taste.

"Enjoy, my friends," he exclaimed before walking away.

She realized Mac was staring at her as she broke off another piece. "What? Do I have something on my face?"

He smiled. "No. Just enjoying the show," he answered before taking a bite of his own.

Chapter Ten

Mac concentrated on the explosion of flavor on his tongue rather than the beautiful woman across from him. It was safer this way. Watching her eat had become his new favorite spectator sport. She took such pleasure, savoring each bite. His sweatpants grew tighter across his lap thinking about it. She wanted a friend right now. Not his baser qualities. He sighed and took another bite.

"Have you ever tasted something this delicious? These past few days I remembered why I love to run. Because I love to eat."

Granted, her too thin frame wasn't the norm, but she didn't strike him as the eat anything she wanted type. "Not a rabbit then?"

He laughed at the look of confusion on her face. "You know, the 'I only eat salads and other heathy stuff' type."

"I love pizza topped with every kind of meat you can think of. Get between me and that, and you might be drawing back a bloodied stump." The gleam in her eye told him she meant it.

"Good to know."

She took another bite, but he could almost hear the wheels turning in her head. "Out with it."

"Fine. I'm wondering how many more preconceived

notions you hold about me. I'd rather get them out of the way now. Then they won't sneak up on me. Go ahead, I can take it."

"I don't have any," he blustered, knowing it wasn't true.

"Sure, you do. Let me help you." She held up a hand and ticked one finger. "Yes, I have someone who cleans for me. Not because I'm spoiled but because life is too short to waste time cleaning. My biggest vice is clothes shopping. Or maybe travel. I also like to get mani-pedis on a regular basis. My mother, bless her heart, tried for years to interest me in cooking without any success. I order out way too much. If I'm not running, then I'm not much of a morning person. On the other hand, I do my own laundry and try to be nice to old ladies and small animals."

He sat back, letting her words wash over him. And found sitting here with her, in a bakery, sweaty and dressed in running clothes seemed ideal. He was happy. "For the record, I know I've been wrong about you. And I'm sorry. I won't make those cracks again. I also hate to clean, but I hate tripping over my own shoes. I do cook, as you know. I'm pretty good, if I do say so myself. Cooking relaxes me."

"My mother says the same thing."

He nodded. "You won't catch me getting a mani pedi anytime soon. And I know what it is because my partner is obsessed. She's a girl, uh, woman."

She reached across the table, covering his hand with one of hers. And he felt it to his toes. "Go on. We're playing a version of my friend Charlie's game, 'What's your favorite flavor'?"

"Charlie Avery? The ER doc?"

"The very one. We go to book club together once a month at Between the Covers. Which usually ends with margaritas somewhere. Although not for Charlie, as she doesn't drink. And not for the pregnant or breastfeeding ones either. I may be the only drinker left." A frown marred her face. "Used to go to book club. Used to love margaritas. I'm getting back to it."

"Ah, the female version of poker and beer night. Charlie's Brendan is part of our crowd. It's grown a bit in the last year, with Flynn and Sebastian moving to town. And there have been a lot of changes there, too. I may be the only single guy left."

"Andrew loved poker night. And I loved that he had you guys. Talked about you all the time." She fell silent.

"It's okay, you know, to talk about him. Not talking about him doesn't make it any better, does it?"

No, it does not. I miss him." She leaned in closer across the table. "Can I tell you something, without you thinking I'm insane?"

"Of course. You can tell me anything." He ignored the pounding of his heart, which said otherwise.

"I dreamed about him yesterday. Mind you, I have before. But this was different. He spoke to me in the dream. Told me what I was doing was right. What he wanted for me. Does it make any sense to you?"

He stared at the furrow between her eyebrows, his fingers itching to soothe it. "It does. I've never lost someone like you have. I won't say I understand. On the other hand, I've never had a great love like you have either. Maybe Shakespeare knew what he was talking about."

"Tennyson wrote it, but you have a point. Maybe. I wouldn't give up the time I had with him for anything." If only there'd been more, she added silently.

"Even knowing how it ends?"

"Yes, even knowing." She let out a short, harsh laugh. "Of course, I would never have chosen this ending."

"Maybe focus on the time you had with him, the quality not quantity."

She blew out a long breath. "Maybe."

"Do you think you could ever love someone again? Fall in love again?"

She remained silent for so long, he almost took it back. But then her face relaxed. "I don't know. I never thought I could love anyone the way I loved him. The totality of it. The completeness. I do know one thing. I'll never settle. All those guys who came before Andrew pale in comparison. It was like I was treading water until I found him. Or he found me. But now I know what love can be. And I won't settle for one drop less if there is a next time."

"Makes sense."

"What about you? How come some woman hasn't snatched you up? Spit out a few mini Macs? Are you one of those confirmed bachelors?"

"Not at all. Like you, I am not willing to settle. I may not have had the great love yet, but she's out there. I know she is."

"Not sweet little Debbie over at Quinn's office?"

He tried to ignore the burning in his ears. "No, not her. She's a baby. And her daddy would shoot me even if I was interested."

She laughed, a light, tinkering sound which soothed the raw edges of his nerves. "Sorry, I couldn't resist. Everyone knows about her mad crush on you."

"The joys of small-town life."

"Tell me about it. But seriously, no one? You must have a long list of qualities to have not found anyone yet."

He shook his head. "No, not really. Sure, there are certain things I like in a woman. Find attractive. But, it's more about the feeling you get when you're with someone. The peace you feel."

"Like you're whole when you didn't know you weren't before."

"Yes." He stopped then, thinking about how he felt with her. It hit a bit too close to home. She didn't want to know.

She must have felt his discomfort, because she changed the subject. "Paige tells me my mother lassoed you into the bachelor auction. How did she manage it?"

"Are you kidding? Have you met your mother? She walked into the station one day and asked a couple of the younger guys, who were very amused when she skipped me. Before you know, I volunteered. Crazy like a fox that one."

She laughed until she had to wipe her eyes on a napkin.

"You fell for the oldest trick in the book, Mac. The old male ego trick. You pegged her right. If it hadn't worked, she would have resorted to batting her eyelashes at you."

He groaned. "Anything but that. And now I have to wear a tux twice!"

"Oh, poor baby. My heart breaks for you. All you have to do is shower, shave and throw on a suit."

"And a tie. You forgot about the tie always making me feel as though I'm choking."

"Wow! But there's no waxing or hours spent on hair and makeup. No killer heels which look great but hurt for days."

"Explain why you do it to me. I never understood why you'd wear something so painful."

"And who do you think designs them? Men of course."

"And who buys them? Women. You can't have it both ways."

"Maybe, maybe not. I'm not going to give up my killer heels. But I'm not going to stop bitching about them either."

"The tux doesn't look so bad when you put it that way."

"See? My work here is done." She popped the last bite of her cinnamon roll into her mouth, her eyes wide as saucers. "I can't believe I ate the whole thing," she muttered behind her hand.

"You needed it. I am a little bummed I don't get to finish it, though."

"I think we both had enough." She gathered the plates and napkins and walked toward the counter. "You did it again, Mr. De Luca. Another hit."

"Of course, my dear. There aren't any losers at De Luca's." He handed her a bag. "A little something for later. Real men like a little flesh on the bones. Am I right, Mac?"

"You're right, sir." He hooked a thumb at Amy. "This one could use a few pounds."

Amy nodded. "Agreed. I have some catching up to do. But then, coming here ought to do the trick."

She kissed the older man's cheek. "Tell Kat I'll see her at the next book club meeting."

Mac swore he saw a tear in the other man's eyes. "I will, dear. My Ekaterina will be thrilled. She's been very worried about you. We all have."

"I know, and I appreciate it. You don't have to worry anymore, Mr. De Luca."

"I can see." He grinned at Mac. "You have chosen well."

She opened her mouth as if to correct him but didn't. "See you soon. And thank you for the gift." She waved the bag and turned toward the door.

Mac stepped around her to open it for her, waiting until they were outside before throwing her a look.

"What?"

"Oh, nothing."

She sighed. "I know. I let him continue to think we were together, as in, you know, together."

"As in more than friends?" he offered.

"Yes." She stopped and placed a hand on his arm. Her light touch burned through his sweatshirt. "Would it be the worst thing in the world to let him think it? Maybe spread it around a bit. Then I would be free of the looks."

"What looks?"

She pulled her mouth into a frown. "You know. The 'it's a shame, she's so young' looks. I know they mean well. Everyone does. But if I'm going to make it back to my real life, I need people to stop treating me with kid gloves. I'm not the first person in town to lose their loved one. Sadly, I won't be the last."

"It's a good sign, you know. The irritation."

"Yes. It means I can feel something again. Something other than the numbing weight of sorrow and loss." She grinned, lighting up her face. "Feels good."

"Great. Glad I can help. If people want to think I'm lucky enough to snag the most beautiful girl in town, I'll take it." He wished he could bite off his tongue. Calling her beautiful got him into trouble yesterday. Go figure.

But she laughed. Until she wrapped her arms around her ribs and struggled for air. And it was the best thing he'd heard in a long time. He joined in because her laugh was so infectious.

After a few moments, she came up for air and threw her arms around him. Her head tucked under his chin. He tried to not think about how good she smelled, even after running. Nor about how her body lined up with his perfectly, making him think of other things he had no business thinking about.

"I know you think I'm mad, Mac. It's okay. I'm not, but I did think I was losing my mind for the longest time. I thought I'd never laugh again. Or enjoy the feel of the sun on my skin without feeling guilty. You've taught me to enjoy the simple things. And so much else." She squeezed him tighter before letting him go.

And he felt the loss of her touch down to his toes. "You needed someone. A friend. Glad I could help."

"I have friends. I have family too. I needed you. I've always believed people come into your life for a reason, when you need them. Do you know what I mean?"

"I do. I've always felt that way about Quinn. I was a different person after high school. Angry. Bitter." He shuffled his feet. "I resented your brother, and your whole family I guess, by extension. Alex always seemed to have everything. Be perfect at everything. The golden boy."

"Annoying, isn't it? But he works damn hard for all of it. It's the part you maybe didn't see clearly. The family name, and yes, the money, only get you so much. And we weren't handed a pile of cash when we became adults. Sure, our education was payed for, and I appreciate not being in debt. But he and I work for everything we have." She smiled, softening her words. "How did Quinn help you?"

"I had chosen the wrong path. Let bitterness drive me. I had a very minor scrape with the law; stupid enough to be in a stolen car. Don't worry, I was just along for the ride. I didn't know my buddy had stolen it. The judge gave me a choice. A second chance. Straighten up and make something of my life or continue down a bad path."

"And you chose the former."

"Yes. My grandmother wasn't having it any other way. I went to school to be an EMT. I met Quinn during a ride along at the station. He's only a couple years older than me, but he already had his act together. We became friends. And then I learned about his dad. How he lost him in the line of duty when Quinn was only a boy. Made my bad choices seem petty."

"And now you save others."

"Very little of what I do is actually saving people's lives, but I do what I can to at least make them better."

"I think Mr. De Luca would disagree. As would his whole family."

"They might. But it's the ones you can't save who haunt you."

"Like Andrew," she whispered, never breaking eye contact.

"Yes, exactly like him." He dropped her gaze, staring at the ground.

"I never blamed you, Mac. I know I haven't handled it well, but I never blamed you."

"I tried, Amy. I need you to know. There was nothing I could do. Couldn't get him to the ER any faster than we did."

"I know. I've always known. But I was too blinded by my grief to think of anyone else. He was never coming home to me again. It's all I could see back then. All I could feel."

"You never got to say goodbye to him. I'm sorry. And I don't know if this helps, but he wasn't alone. Quinn and I stayed with him. Quinn kneeled on the floor, holding his hand the whole way to the hospital. I had to tell him to move when I needed access. But we never left him." He cleared his throat. "And he spoke about you. With his last breaths, his thoughts centered around you. He made Quinn promise to tell you he loved you and was sorry. Sorry for breaking his promise to you."

She closed her eyes for a long moment then blinked. "I didn't know. Thank you for telling me. Quinn and I have never, uh, talked about that day. I wouldn't let him." Her somber gaze held his. "Maybe I should have. I like knowing he had you guys." She dropped her gaze, hands tightening on the bakery bag. "I should go now."

"Okay. I'm working over the weekend, so maybe next week? Monday? At our bench?"

"Sure." She gave him a small smile and turned away.

He watched her walk away until she turned a corner and he couldn't see her anymore. He hoped his words had done some good and not caused more pain for her. It was the last thing he would ever want to do.

Chapter Eleven

On Saturday afternoon, Amy twirled in the mirror to a chorus of oohs and aahs. What started as she and Paige dress hunting for her had grown into quite the party. Since Windsor Falls remained a small town, Infatuations was the only choice. But it was all she had needed. The small clothing boutique offered everything from upscale casual to to-die-for formal. And everything in between. Already, a row of long dresses in silver and black hung in her dressing room, awaiting their turn to shine. Elizabeth and Katie, who knew the owner, Lisa, from high school had suggested it and come along. Then Charlie and Jamie heard about the event and showed up. Amy wasn't sure who brought the champagne. Kat brought a selection of delicious pastries made for just the occasion.

"This is the one," Paige called out around a mouthful of cracker crumbs. Morning sickness had spread into the afternoon.

Amy grinned at her friend. "Same thing you said about the last dress."

"And the one before that," called out Charlie. "Although I did agree with her that time. The daring side slit made your legs look even longer than they are already."

The half dozen women present all added their thoughts, which swirled around Amy, comforting her in a friendly haze.

She'd missed this. These women. This town. For so long, she'd buried herself in grief so deep she may as well have been buried right alongside Andrew. And he wouldn't want that for her. She didn't want it for her. Not anymore. She wanted to live. To feel the sunshine on her skin. To surround herself with these lovely women.

"This might be the one," she murmured, her voice lost in the increasing din of her friends. She fingered the shining material, loving the way it caressed her frame. The spaghetti straps showed off her neck and cleavage without being too much. The slit to mid-thigh on her left leg rivaled the one Charlie mentioned. Her skin seemed to glow in the silvery tone. She piled her hair on top of her head, twisting side to side, to get some ideas.

And forgot to breathe. She caught sight of Mac standing outside, gazing at her. She only had a second to compose herself before a bell tinkered over the door.

"Hello, ladies," Mac called out. A chorus of greetings followed. He walked up to Paige, bending to kiss her cheek. "Are the crackers working?"

"Barely, but I'm not complaining. They're all I can stand some days. This wasn't the way I envisioned losing the last stubborn twenty pounds."

"The twenty pounds looks great on you. Don't let anyone tell you otherwise."

She didn't turn, didn't acknowledge him but watched in the mirror as he made the rounds. Not once did he seem to think he might be out of place. But with his graceful stride, a word here, a chuckle there, he wasn't. When he had spoken to everyone, he approached the dais on which she stood, surrounded by mirrors.

"I haven't seen the others, but this one gets my vote."

She raised one brow, never breaking eye contact with him in the mirror. "I'll take it under advisement."

His warm, hearty chuckle sent a shiver down the length of her spine, curling her bare toes. He winked and turned away. "Don't worry, ladies. I'll let you get back to it." And then he was gone.

"How is that man still single?" came a question from the group, followed by several sighs.

"I thought everyone here was either married or spoken for," Amy tossed over her shoulder.

"I'm not," called Jaime.

"I'm married not dead," yelled Katie.

"Same," agreed Kat. "Well, not married but spoken for anyway."

Amy stayed silent on the subject but agreed. Why *was* he still single? A man with his own house, a great job, intelligent and charming. Guys liked him; women sighed over him. What was his deal?

"Why is he still single?" she asked before she could stop herself. And wished she could crawl back into the dressing room. "I'm only curious," she muttered.

"A question for the ages," answered Elizabeth.

"He's not gay, if that's what you're asking," offered Jaime.

"Oh, I know he's not."

Silence reigned. *She really had to learn to keep her mouth shut.*

"And how do you know? Do tell!" encouraged Katie.

She held her head high, tried to draw upon her Windsorness. And failed miserably. "Uh, I mean I don't know, of course. He doesn't seem gay." She stopped talking before she had to insert her foot past mid-thigh.

"Give the girl a break," commanded Paige. She made her way through the crowd of giggling women. Spinning Amy to face them, she grinned. "Ladies, I do believe we have a winner. Amy, what do you think?"

She looked out at the sea of expectant faces and then down at herself and over her shoulder into the mirror. And nodded. A roar filled the small store. "Now, all I need are the perfect shoes and purse to match."

"I have what you need," answered Lisa, the boutique owner. She handed Amy a pair of darling, strappy silver sandals with the right amount of heel. She slid her feet into them, doing up the buckle on each. The first thing that popped into her head was Mac would still be taller than her. And she smiled.

*****

Across town, Trina eyed her partner above her cheeseburger. "What's gotten into you? You're smiling. It's creepy."

Mac tossed off her comments and took another bite of his grilled chicken sandwich. He washed it down with a gulp of soda before answering her. "What? I can't smile now? Didn't know you had rules."

"No offense, but you've been a bit of a bear at times lately. What gives? Does this have anything to do with a certain blonde?"

He fashioned his mouth into a sloppy grin. "Oh, have you seen the new retriever puppy the captain got? She's a real cutie," he joked.

"Not that blonde," she mumbled before throwing her balled up napkin at his head. "You know who I mean."

"I do and no comment." He took another huge bite, as though it sealed the deal. But he knew his partner better. She wouldn't let it go.

"Where did you disappear to on the way here?"

"I stopped into Infatuations to say hello to Paige and her friends. Seems the wedding planning has been kicked into high gear."

"Ah ha," she crowed, stealing one of his fries. "I knew it."

"Knew what?"

"I knew your improved mood had something to do with Amy Windsor."

"Amy is just my friend." He crossed his fingers under the table. His Granny would skin him alive for lying. If she were here. It wasn't exactly a lie, he consoled himself. They were becoming friends. Slowly. Mile by mile, as it were. And if she made him smile by being within a hundred yards, so be it.

He'd deal with the rest another time.

"Friends, huh?"

He wasn't off the hook. Just off it for now. He'd take it. And because he loved Trina like the little sister he'd never had, he dropped a handful of fries on her plate. "Another in a long line of mysteries about women. If you wanted fries, why order the broccoli?"

She speared a piece of the vegetable. "Because broccoli is healthy. And I like it." She popped it in her mouth, chewing and swallowing, as if to prove her point. Then she did the same with a fry. "But I also love fries. Especially yours."

Mac shook his head at his partner's 'logic' and snagged a few of them as well. He hadn't known what to think of the tiny spitfire when they'd been paired a few years ago. But what she lacked in size, Trina made up for in mouth and attitude. And a heart the size of North Carolina. She was smart and thought on her feet, a necessary trait for the job. And their patients loved her. Yes, he'd won the partner lottery. Not that he was telling her.

"Quinn and Paige are finally getting hitched. I never thought it would happen," she commented.

"They worked it out."

"And somehow you're taking credit?"

"Well, I did nudge Amy along."

"Bulldoze is more like it."

"I said what she needed to hear."

"She just didn't know it at the time."

"Yes. Exactly."

She shook her head and got up to pay the check.

"What?" he called to her retreating back.

"Never mind."

"Women," he muttered to himself as he threw down some bills to cover the tip.

"Amen," called a man in a booth he passed. Mac grinned and hurried to catch up to her.

Chapter Twelve

Monday morning, the swiftly approaching winter bared its teeth, producing the chilliest running yet. Days like this could convince her running on a treadmill, in a climate-controlled room, might not be the worst thing ever. Amy jogged in place while she waited for him, not wanting to lose the warm-up she'd already done. She glanced at her phone. He had exactly one minute before she called it and returned to her lovely, welcoming down comforter.

"I know! I'm here!" the man in question yelled, running across Evergreen Avenue toward her. Windsor Fall's version of Main Street USA beckoned to her. Already, people milled about in De Luca's Bakery and Cup O' Joe next door. Nice warm places she'd rather be right now.

She glanced up at the leaden sky. No hope of even the weakest winter sun there for warmth. "You're lucky," she said by way of greeting when he joined her. She continued to blow hot air against her gloved hands, rubbing them in hopes of a little heat. "As much as I love my mountains, a tropical beach is sounding pretty good right now."

Mac nodded, his even, white teeth flashing as he smiled. "Agreed. Sorry I'm late. Ready?" He took off running rather than wait for a reply.

She laughed and sprinted to catch up. "I'll have you know

I was knee-deep in a fantasy concerning my downed comforter when you deigned to show."

Mac stumbled, taking a few strides to regain his rhythm. "Well played," he yelled to her over his shoulder. "There's an image I'll carry around for quite some time."

She felt the blood rush to her face and kept her eyes straight ahead. Then realized that put them straight on his butt. And even in baggy winter sweats, it was a sight to behold. And then it was her turn to stumble. *Mind out of the gutter, Amy. You're not ready to think about anyone like that again. Especially not him.* Lecture over, she made up the ground between them, running at his left elbow.

"What, no sassy comeback?"

She shook her head, preferring to not speak. Better to concentrate on running and breathing in the freezing temperature. Also, better for keeping one's foot out of one's mouth.

"You disappoint me. I've come to enjoy our little give and take." He shrugged his shoulders. "Did you take my advice?" He pulled ahead slightly. So much for *not* checking out his butt.

"Advice?" What advice could she have gotten from him?

"About the dress. Did you choose the shiny one I saw you in on Saturday?"

More blood rushed her face as she remembered locking eyes with him in the boutique mirror. "Yes, I did. But not because you liked it. It happened to be my favorite." She refrained, barely, from sticking out her tongue at him. She needed to keep some dignity.

"And out of curiosity, how many others did you try on after the one I saw?"

"None," she ground out between clenched molars.

"And how many prior?" His chuckle burst forth in a puff of steam.

"I have a better question. Are you gay?"

This time, he almost went down in a heap. As did she. He stopped abruptly, causing Amy to collide into the solid wall of his back. Her arms pinwheeled as she tried to stop herself from falling over backwards. She would have, if not for his quick thinking. Mac twisted, grabbing each of her arms in one of his hands.

They stood there, inches apart, both breathing, neither talking. She focused on the mechanics of it. In. Out. And avoided his gaze. Until he drew up her chin with one long finger under it. "What makes you think I'm gay?"

"I, uh, don't. It came up in conversation. After you left on Saturday."

His eyes widened, as did his smile. "Really? How?"

She struggled to hold his gaze, desperate to look anywhere but. "You know, because you're still single and all."

"So, I must be gay?"

She swallowed. Hard. "Uh, sort of." And struggled to not cross her fingers against the blatant lie. "Everyone wanted to know how you're still single when you're such a nice guy," she blurted out in one long breath.

"Nice," he repeated as if she had called him a serial killer.

"There are worse things than being nice."

"I'm almost afraid to ask, but how did my sexual orientation come into it?"

"I might have offered you didn't seem gay to me. Not that I would have a problem if you were," she added in a rush.

The darkening of his eyes was her only warning. He dropped her arms, closed the distance between them, and placed his lips on hers. No other parts of their bodies touched. For a second, his firm lips chilled hers. But only for a second. Her eyes drifted closed as a rush of warmth spread from the single point of contact, igniting a fire within her. She swayed toward him, seeking the warmth he offered. A faint but distinct growl sprang from him. And he broke the contact.

"Any doubts left?"

She opened her eyes, struggling to focus on his. "No. Not a one."

"Good. Let's get going." And he started to run again.

She growled this time. But for an entirely different reason.

*****

"You'll never believe what that man did this time. Call me as soon as you can." She finished her message to Paige and ended the call. Hours later, she still smarted from his little trick. If it was a trick. One didn't get to their late twenties without recognizing interest from a man. But it had been a long time. And part of her life died with Andrew. Hadn't it? She touched a hand to her lips, reliving the brief yet exquisite contact. The warmth and chills had enveloped her. Then shook her head in disgust. Surely, she wasn't standing in the middle of her condo mooning over Mac!

Fueled by the thought, she stomped out to her car and dragged another suitcase from the trunk. Moving back in day had arrived. Not that she had known when she awoke this morning. But it was time. Past time. She'd gone back to her parents' home after her run and made a snap decision. Her poor mother had acted as though she were shipping out to war, rather than moving less than ten minutes away. But Amy had also seen relief and pride behind the tears in her mother's eyes. And a small layer of the weight she'd carried since Andrew's death fell away.

She brought the suitcase into her bedroom, hoisting it onto the bed. As she unpacked, she thought about the unexpected phone call she'd received from her old boss earlier in the morning. The school principal had never been Amy's biggest fan. Nor Paige's. In her sixties and approaching retirement, Mrs. Morton preferred things to be done 'the way they've always been done.' Amy secretly thought she meant the old adage, 'children are to be seen and not heard' but never raised the courage to ask.

One of the second-grade teachers had tried skiing over the weekend. Without a lot of success. One fractured wrist and a minor surgery later, she was expected to be out all week. They'd found coverage for today, but was Amy interested in substituting the rest of the week? She agreed before even thinking about it. This was what she wanted. To get back to her life.

The call coming from Mrs. Morton and not the scheduling office also came as a shock. But the older woman, always distant and strict, had shown Amy a crack in her ever-present armor after Andrew died. Several months after his death, Amy had received a card with a hand-written letter. She'd lost her young husband in a far-off land, fighting a war he didn't understand. They'd married the day before he left for combat. She'd never married again.

Sharing something like this with her softened her image of her former boss. Made her human. She knew better than to ever share the news with anyone. She hadn't even told Paige out of some sense of loyalty or bond with Mrs. Morton. But she carried the knowledge with her. And she'd be teaching second grade this week. The thought made her groan aloud. She preferred her six-year-olds. But it was only for a few days. And she'd been assured lesson plans were already in place. What could go wrong?

Several hours later and back from a grocery store run, a knock sounded at her door. She opened it to Paige juggling a bottle of wine and a lovely bouquet of flowers. A huge smile wreathed her face before she threw her laden arms around Amy. "You're coming back!" she yelled and bounced at the same time.

"Wow, word travels fast in a small town."

"Even faster in a small elementary school. And now I need your bathroom." She fled in that direction before Amy could even shut the front door.

She walked into the kitchen and found a vase for the flowers. The bright blues and purples cheered her still sterile feeling home. She let out a shaky breath. She could do this. At least the fridge and cabinets were stocked with easy things to make. The rest would come, she assured herself.

"Whew. I feel better now."

"Since your skin isn't carrying its ever-present green tinge, I'm assuming that was about your bladder, not your stomach."

"Give the lady a Kewpie doll," she smirked and pulled out the ever-present sleeve of bland crackers. "And to be safe, I'll have a few of these. I've discovered always having a little something in my belly seems to help." She plopped down at the breakfast bar that divided the miniscule kitchen from the living area. "Now, to the good stuff. What did Mac do this time to annoy you?"

"He kissed me," Amy blurted before covering her mouth with a hand. And would have laughed at her friend's huge eyes if she wasn't feeling shaky.

"I might need another cracker," Paige joked before shoving in several and chewing. "Okay, tell me everything."

And she did. The run. The mild flirting. And then the conversation from Saturday about his not being gay.

"No! You didn't! You told him you thought he was gay?" A very Paige specific snort erupted from her friend. "I would have given anything to be a fly on the wall."

She thought about fixing her with the patented Windsor stare, but it wouldn't have worked on her oldest friend, who was an honorary Windsor herself. Not to mention Mac being gay *was* ludicrous. She laughed instead. Until she wrapped her arms around her ribs and struggled for air. "I did," she croaked in return.

"And he kissed you?"

She nodded, wiping her eyes.

"Wow! Was it as good as I imagine it was?"

"Paige!"

"Amy! The man is hot. H. O. T." She rubbed her lower abdomen. "And this little jellybean has me awash in a sea of hormones. Ask Quinn." She grinned. "He's not complaining."

"Eww, I will not ask him that."

"Spoilsport. Can you imagine his face if you did? But back to Mac." She held up one hand, ticking off fingers as she went. "He's taller than you. Has shoulders that go on for miles. He's funny and smart. He cares about people and small animals. He's single. Should I start on the other hand?"

Amy shook her head. "But, he's not Andrew." And all the oxygen left the room.

Paige's expressive face crumbled. "No, he's not," she said, wiping a tear. "But no one ever will be, Amy."

"You're right, of course. I know you are. And for one quick moment, it felt...nice. Better than nice if I'm being honest."

Paige squeezed her hand. "Baby steps. Andrew has been gone for a year and a half. And a guy came along who caught your interest. It's not the end of the world. It doesn't have to even be a big deal. Unless you want it to."

"Of course not." Amy jumped up and paced around the table. "Honestly, we've been hanging out, but he makes me crazy. He lectures me and calls me 'princess.'" And brings a smile to her face, something she'd lacked for too long. And listened to her talk about Andrew. But she wasn't sharing with the class.

"Maybe a little crazy is what you need right now. Nothing serious. Nothing that has to be the start of anything. Have a little fun. And Mac is fun. And delicious."

"Paige!"

"Not even going to apologize. Just stating the facts. You heard everyone after he left on Saturday. I'm not the only one who feels this way."

"No, you're not." Present company included if their kiss held any indication. But she wasn't giving away this little nugget of information either.

But she and Paige formed a bond before they were born. Her friend stopped, tilted her head, and looked at her. Funny. With the slightest of smiles tugging the corners of her mouth.

"You like him." She clapped her hands before dropping them in her lap. "Oh, you like him."

"I do not," she protested, getting up to pace. "And what are you, twelve? Okay, I like him as in he's a decent guy who's been nice to me. I don't like him like him." She stopped, staring at the wall above Paige's shoulder. "Not like that," she all but whispered. She let out a shaky breath and collapsed onto her chair. "I can't."

"Sure, you can. Baby steps, Amy. You take it a day at a time, see what happens. See if something develops between you."

"It's not like he asked me out. One kiss, Paige. Quite a kiss. But one kiss." She stopped, staring at her friend, hands over her mouth. Too late.

Paige pumped her fist in the air. "I knew it," she crowed.

"Nice," muttered Amy.

"Why? Was it terrible? Oh, did he use too much tongue? Eww, why do guys think it's a good thing? It shouldn't feel as though a Saint Bernard is licking your face."

"It wasn't terrible. There wasn't any tongue. He kissed me so softly. I was freezing. Then I wasn't."

"Oh. That kind of kiss. Nice."

Amy waved a hand between them. "No matter. It won't happen again. Can't." And the thought brought down the corners of her smile.

"And why not?" Paige crunched another cracker, waiting for her reply. "It doesn't have to mean anything, Amy. You could get your feet wet again."

"He's your about to be husband's close friend, not some random guy I won't see again. I can't have an affair with Mac. He's an important part of your life."

Paige rubbed her gently rounded abdomen. "Not to mention the future godfather of my future baby."

"Exactly! Especially since I better be this nugget's future godmother."

"Of course, you are. Who else would I choose?"

Amy sighed, slipping onto the couch. She tucked her feet under her. "Then you see my point. We live in a small town, where almost everyone knows each other. I can't 'scratch an itch' per se with him." She shook her head. "This conversation is ridiculous. I'm not having sex anytime soon. With anyone. Least of all him."

"If you say so," responded her friend.

Paige's very mild tone set off warning bells in her head.

"I'm serious, Paige."

"I heard you," she smirked, nibbling on another cracker.

"Besides, I have twenty-two second graders to prepare for. And all of this." She waved her arm around her apartment.

"Well, I'd stay and help you, but I have a dinner date."

"Someone I know?"

"Oh, only the most handsome man in Windsor Falls." She grinned at Amy and hugged her before letting herself out.

Amy grabbed her laptop from the pile of stuff brought from her mother's house. She turned it on and waited. Mrs. Graff, the other second grade teacher, had promised to send her lesson plans to give Amy an idea of what she'd be teaching this week.

Which reminded her. No running with Mac for the rest of the week. She ignored the pang in her stomach. She'd thrown herself in the deep end, taking on a bunch of eight-year-olds for four days when she hadn't taught since last year. Besides, she needed a break from him. From them. Not that there was a them. He was too much right now. Too big. Too macho. *Too attractive.*

Before she could talk herself out of it, Amy dashed off a quick text to him.

Picked up a temporary assignment at school for the rest of the week. Won't be running. Sorry.

She agonized over the wording. What did she have to be sorry about? And then hit send before she drove herself crazy. And to save what remained of her sanity, she turned off the ringer and blasted her running playlist. Nothing like a little motivation to unpack.

A few hours later, happy but exhausted, Amy placed the last suitcase, thankfully empty, in her closet before flopping down on her newly made bed. There. She'd done it. She'd moved back in, reclaimed her home for her own. And if Andrew's spirit still lingered, she'd deal with it.

Her stomach growled, reminding her she'd forgotten lunch. She made her way to the kitchen when a knock on her door changed her direction. She smiled, knowing her mother couldn't resist bringing her home-made meals.

"I can cook, you know, Mama. Lucky for you, I am very hungry," she joked as she swung open the door.

"I'm glad you're hungry, but I'm not your mother."

Chapter Thirteen

The smile, followed by a creep of pink across her cheek bones, warmed Mac's heart. He extended the pizza box he held. "I may not be your mother, but I do come bearing food."

"I can see."

"May I come in?"

The pink deepened. *Interesting.*

"Of course." Amy stepped back to allow him to enter, giving him a wide berth. Also, interesting.

"Luckily for you, meat lovers happens to also be my favorite." He moved past her, giving her space. For now. The kiss they'd shared remained on his mind. He wanted another taste but didn't want to scare her off.

"As long as you skipped the anchovies." She wrinkled her nose. "Never could stand the idea of fish on my pizza." She moved to the kitchen table. "Not that I don't appreciate this, but to what do I owe the honor?"

"I got your text. And I thought maybe the idea of going back to teaching tomorrow might be making you a bit nervous. Plus, you have to eat, and I figured you might be busy with preparations for your first day back."

He panicked for a moment when her eyes grew larger. Then she hugged him. Hard. And stepped out of his reach before he could react.

"Thank you. This was very kind of you. And I never say no to pizza."

"First nice, now kind. You're killing me." He took off his coat and threw it over the back of her couch. "I'm on my way in, which is why I'm dressed like this."

She looked him up and down, from his shiny black work boots to his uniform shirt. "I thought you worked days."

"I do. But Paul's wife is due like yesterday. It's their first, and she's anxious when he's gone. I told him I'd cover for him tonight."

She smirked at him before opening the fridge. "See? Both kind and nice apply," she commented to the depths of the appliance.

The yoga pants might be loose, but they gave an impression of what lay beneath. His thoughts were neither kind nor nice.

"Were you checking out my butt?"

"Guilty," he replied without even a hint of it.

"Guess that makes us even." She handed him a bottled water and sat at the table.

What? He sat across from her and grabbed two slices. Chewing and swallowing gave him a moment to think of a reply.

"What did you think of it? My butt?"

She took a long drink of water before answering. "Not bad."

"Damned with faint praise."

"You were wearing heavy winter sweats. It's not like I could see. Much."

"I see." But he didn't. Was she flirting with him? "Tell me about going back to work. How do you feel?"

"Great. Terrified." She laughed. "Both. It's been awhile. And I've only taught the younger ones." She put down her slice of pizza, placing her hands in her lap.

"I'm sorry. I wasn't trying to make you nervous. Or to feel badly."

She smiled at him, and he felt it right in his gut. "Oh no,

you didn't. It's uh, a lot. You know?" She waved a hand to indicate the apartment. "First day back here as well."

More than anything, he wanted to go to her. Wrap his arms around her and whisper everything would be fine. But he didn't know if it would. "You're doing the right thing. Getting back into it." His eyes sought hers. He smiled encouragement.

"You're right. And I know this past year has been, well, self-indulgent." She shook her head, the thousand shades of blonde catching the light. "I'll be okay."

"You'll do the best you can. It's all anyone can ask. And I think it will get easier. Maybe a little bit, every day."

She blew out a breath. "Being back here, in my home, without him. Well, it's rough. I think I'll hear his key in the door. The sound of his boots hitting the floor when he takes them off."

"I can't imagine. I miss him, too, and I know what you mean. Sometimes, I forget. I start to call or text him. Then, I remember."

She reached across the table and covered his hand with hers. "Yes. I do it, too."

The gesture was meant to give him comfort. He knew that. But the touch of her skin on his sent a rush through him. An electrical impulse scorched him from within. "I know my grief is not the same as yours. But I do miss him." He turned his hand over until he could grip hers. Gently, almost tentatively. He didn't want to scare her.

They sat with their fingers loosely entwined for a few moments. And then she drew her hand back and picked up her pizza. "I haven't cried," she mumbled around the slice.

"You haven't?" The memory of her at the funeral swam to the surface. Perfect makeup and not a hair out of place in swamp like heat. And not a single tear. He remembered thinking her face might crack from the tension in it.

She shook her head slowly. "Not since the day Quinn came to tell me." She looked at him, with huge eyes, and he wanted to enfold her in his arms again. "I cried so much the day he died. I couldn't stop. They sedated me. Then, nothing. Not even a single tear since. What's wrong with me?"

Her tone, devoid of any emotion, did him in. He got up and moved to the chair next to hers. Then he took her in his arms, cradling her face against his chest. "There's nothing wrong with you, Amy. You've suffered a terrible loss. And I'm no expert, but I think everyone finds their own way through. Not crying is your way."

She shuddered against him then settled in a little more. "It's like standing in the ocean, a smooth, calm one. You're fine. And then a rogue wave comes from nowhere and knocks you over. That's what my grief feels like."

Mac stroked her long hair, trying anything to make her feel better. Safe. Cared for. He tucked her head under his chin. "Sounds about right. But are the waves getting further apart?"

"A little," she mumbled into his chest.

"Good." He pressed his lips into her hair.

"The forgetting, even for a moment like you said, is the worst. Sometimes, I wake up. And for a moment, before I even open my eyes, I forget. Just for a second. And then it comes back to me. The awful truth. He's gone. I'll never see him again."

"I'm sorry," he whispered into her hair. "I wish I could take away your pain."

She hugged him then sat up. Her dry eyes stared into him. "I know you do, Mac. And a part of me wishes you could. But this is my life. And I'm taking it back, bit by bit. Moving back in here might have been the hardest bit, but it had to be done."

"Agreed."

"And tomorrow, I'll go back to work. Having Paige down the hall will help. So will having a routine." She smiled at him. "Not that I don't appreciate the morning run."

"We could go really early."

"Not this week. I have to throw myself into teaching. Do it right. Those kids deserve one hundred percent."

"You'll be fine." He gave her hand a squeeze and stood, glancing at his watch. "I'd better go."

"Okay. Thanks again for dinner."

"I brought pizza, Amy, not a gourmet meal."

"You brought me food and more importantly company when you knew I'd need both." She went up on her toes and kissed his cheek. "I appreciate both."

"You're welcome. Let me know how tomorrow goes." He crossed his fingers, waved them at her, and walked out.

*****

Amy stood there, long after he'd left. It took every ounce of willpower not to call him back. Ask him to stay. For those few moments, wrapped in his arms, she'd felt safe. Calm. Cherished. Whole. She hadn't felt those in a long time. Not since Andrew. She shook her head at the ridiculousness of the thought. Putting away the leftover pizza, Amy replayed the moments in her mind. The man made her crazy, one minute calling her out, the next comforting her. He wasn't someone to get involved with, to lean on. He was a distraction. Someone to help her find her way back to the living. Amuse her. Call her on her BS. That's all he could be. And yet, for a moment, he felt like something else. A possibility.

She rinsed the dishes before placing them in the dishwasher then headed into her bedroom. Stopping in the doorway, she surveyed the room, steeling herself. Last time she'd slept in here, Andrew lay at her side. And he never would again. Maybe if she repeated it to herself enough times, it would feel real.

She sat on the bed and booted up her laptop. An email from the other second grade teacher caught her notice. Sure enough, she'd attached the lesson plans needed for the week. Amy said a silent prayer of thanks and clicked on the attachment, then rubbed her sweaty palms along her thighs. Second and kindergarten might only be two years apart in age, but in curriculum, they were light years away from each other. *You can do this.*

The next two hours flew as she immersed herself in the

world of second grade curriculum. The structure of their day leant itself to more actual teaching than playing like she did with the younger set. What with all the reading, math, science, and social studies, Amy rubbed her temples. She shut down her computer and placed it on the nightstand, plugged in, to be ready for tomorrow.

You can do this. She said her mantra aloud to herself again, hoping the words rang true tomorrow. Then she got ready for bed. More than anything, she needed a good night's sleep if she wanted to get through the next few days. And she wanted much more.

Stuffing her laptop in her backpack, Amy raced to the door the next morning. After tossing and turning for a chunk of the night, she'd almost overslept. She'd have to worry about breakfast, not to mention caffeine, somewhere along the way. She wanted to arrive early, give herself time to acclimate to the classroom.

She locked her door and flew down the hall to the front door of the old Victorian house. And came to a dead stop at the sight of Mac standing on the porch, coffee and a takeout sack from Bob's in hand.

"The coffee is black. Plain but very strong stuff." He raised the brown bag. "As for breakfast, I went for a mixture of protein and sugar."

She cut off anything else he might have said with a smacking kiss on the lips. "You're amazing. I just cursed myself for not getting up in time for a decent breakfast." She grabbed the coffee cup and took a big sip. "Not to mention the caffeine. You're the best."

She smothered a giggle at the sight of the red creeping across his prominent cheekbones.

"It's nothing. I wanted you to have a good first day."

"And now, thanks to you, I will. But I have to go."

"No worries. I'll walk you to your car." He covered a huge yawn as they walked. "Nightshift never fails to knock me on my ass."

She juggled everything she was holding and clicked open her door. "Did you get any sleep?"

"Not so much. Some black ice out on the highway took care of that. Luckily, nothing too serious, but we were out there for a few hours. Then there was one fire standby and several minor medical calls."

"Wow. No wonder you're tired. It makes me tired thinking about it." She glanced at her phone and cursed under her breath. "I really have to go. But thank you for breakfast. Very thoughtful."

"You were on my way home. Have a good first day back."

"I hope to. At least Paige will be right down the hall. Knowing her, she'll be checking on me every hour."

"That's what best friends are for. See you." He gave a small wave before jogging to his truck.

Amy watched him go then sat in her car and pulled the door closed. She started it and waited for the windows to defrost as she opened her unexpected breakfast. He'd thought of everything. In the paper bag sat a bacon and egg bagel sandwich. She wolfed down the sandwich, washing it down with the strong coffee. She owed him big time.

Fifteen minutes later, Amy pulled in next to Paige's car at Windsor Falls Elementary. She turned off her engine and stared at the building. The knotting of her stomach couldn't be blamed on hunger. *You can do this.* After repeating her mantra, Amy braced herself and got out. She hurried across the icy parking lot, bending her head against the slice of wind threatening to steal her breath. Crossing her fingers for luck, she pulled open the front door.

Chapter Fourteen

Mac stepped out of the shower and swiped a hand across the steamy mirror. He glanced in it, grimacing at the lines of fatigue on his face. It had been awhile since he'd pulled a night shift. And a busy one. Paul owed him. A smile spread across his tired face as he remembered the look of surprise and then delight on Amy's face this morning. With the way his shift had gone, he hadn't been sure he'd get to her house on time to deliver breakfast.

He brushed his teeth before climbing into bed without putting on any clothing. His bedroom was chilly; the way he preferred to sleep. Even with freezing temperatures outside, the ceiling fan turned above his head. Curling up on one side, Mac closed his eyes, more than ready for the escape of sleep.

Despite his fatigue, it didn't come right away. He wondered about Amy. Was she settling in okay today? Was she scared? Excited? Would she be glad she took the assignment? Would this lead to her going back full-time? Did he have the right to ask any of those questions?

He flipped his pillow for the cooler side and thought about the last one. Less than a month ago, she wouldn't look at him, let alone have a conversation. Now they were friends maybe. And then, there was the kiss. And the moments he'd held her in his arms. Something brewed between them.

Something more than 'just friends.' Something he'd love to explore further.

Mac flipped over to his back, sprawling in the middle of the king-sized bed. He pushed the comforter to his waist, suddenly too warm. *Imagine that.* Amy seemed like a wounded animal at times. She was better, coming back to herself, then something set her back. He didn't want to push too hard. Too fast. But he was curious. She'd responded to him. Kissed him back. Even if briefly.

Frustrated, he shoved the pillows out of the way, flipping to his stomach. Should he ask her out on a real date? Not just breakfast after a run. Would she go? Was she ready? In the past two weeks, it seemed as though she'd awoken from a long sleep. She'd lost the dark circles under her eyes. Her hair shone with new health. She even looked like she'd put back on a few pounds. But being a smart man, he wouldn't be mentioning it.

But if she was returning to her old self, Amy Windsor of the Windsor Falls founding family, what would she want with *him*? They'd never ran in the same circles, even in their small hometown. Why would it be any different now? Yet, she seemed different to him. More down to earth. Not the princess he'd always thought her to be. Was it possible he'd done this? Kept her so high on some other plain in his mind and missed the truth?

His eyes drooped. Mac slid into a dreamless sleep with a slight smile on his face.

*****

Amy grabbed a chair at one of the tables in the teacher's lounge and waited for Paige to appear. She smiled again at the banner welcoming her back to work. No doubt also Paige's doing. She blew out a deep breath and opened the container with her salad.

"There you are," exclaimed her best friend. Paige crossed the crowded room and collapsed in a chair next to her.

"Whew, what a morning." She stifled a yawn. "I have no idea how I will keep this up when I'm really pregnant." A smile lit her whole face as she caressed her barely there baby bump. "How are you? How did it go?"

"Not bad, all things considered. Having most of them for kindergarten two years ago helped I think." She took a bite of her lunch, mulling over the morning. "Yep, all in all, not bad."

"Great!" She reached over to squeeze her in a one-armed hug. "That's wonderful, Amy."

"Having the lesson plans certainly helped."

"Of course, but you would have been fine. Kids love you."

"Having a good breakfast first helped." She told Paige about her unexpected early morning visitor. Then sat back and waited for the reaction. She didn't wait long.

"Amy!" Both women looked around at the curious stares. Paige lowered her voice. "Why didn't you tell me?"

"I just did."

"I meant earlier. He showed up with breakfast?"

"And dinner last night." She stopped, laughing at the look on her best friend's face. "Oh, did I not mention it?"

"No, you did not, as you well know." She pointed at her with her fork for good measure. The piece of honeydew threatened to fall

Amy sighed, knowing Paige would make more of it than there was. "I had texted him, letting him know I'd be here all week and not running. And he came by with pizza."

"Awwwwwww."

"Pizza, Paige. Not dinner in Paris."

"Still. That was very sweet of him. Hmmm."

"No, there's no 'hmmm.'"

"Oh, I don't know. First, he brings you dinner and then breakfast. It's not like y'all are dating." Her Cheshire-like grin spoke otherwise. "Are you?"

"No, of course not." But even to her own ears, her answer sounded weak at best.

"And you'd tell me if you were?"

"Of course, Paige. I tell you everything."

She didn't answer but concentrated on her sandwich.

"Paige?"

Her friend looked up but didn't make direct eye contact. "You used to. Before Andrew died."

Amy sucked in a breath, not sure how to answer. She had never considered how her self-imposed exile might have affected her friend. She reached over, squeezing one of her hands. "I'm sorry," she whispered. "I didn't have anything to say for a long time."

Her heart clenched at the tears gathering in her friend's eyes.

Paige made a noise, half sob, half laugh. "Don't mind me. I cry at the drop of a hat these days." She dabbed her eyes on a napkin. "Amy, you shut me out. You shut everyone out. We, I, didn't know how to help you. How to even reach you."

"It hurt so much, losing Andrew. I thought the pain would kill me. Then I didn't feel anything. I went numb. And it was better, in a way. I didn't want to feel anything. And if I talked to you, about him, I feared the pain would return."

Tears flowed freely now. "But I could have, uh, well, I don't know but something."

Amy shook her head. "No, you couldn't have." She hugged her friend. Paige had always been the best person she knew. Wanted to fix everything for everybody. "You couldn't fix me, honey."

"I know," she whispered. "I missed you, Amy."

The two women sat there, staring at each other, for a long moment. Amy's heart ached for what she had put Paige through. "I love you for wanting to help. To make it bearable. I had to do it myself. It was my journey." She heaved a sigh. "And I feel better now. More like my old self. Maybe not a hundred percent, but I'm getting there."

"And Mac is helping."

She couldn't help smiling at her persistence. "Yes, Mac is helping."

"Good. Now tell me about second grade." She picked up

her sandwich, taking a bite.

"Do you remember Danny Cartwright?"

Amy grimaced.

"Yep. He hasn't changed a bit. Still won't keep his mouth closed. Still starting all the trouble."

"Remember when he shoved not one, but two, crayons up his nose?"

"How could I forget? He had them so far up there, you had to call his parents. I'd rather that. Now he picks on people. There's a new kid in class. He's very shy. Just moved here from up north. Danny seems to have made it his personal mission to torment him."

Paige's nostrils flared. "Oh, I cannot tolerate bullying. And at such a young age."

"Exactly. I only have them for a few days, but I am determined to get to the bottom of it."

They finished their lunches, chatting about everything and nothing. Amy's heart swelled in her chest at the familiarity of it. This simple thing, eating lunch with Paige, made her day. Hell, her whole week.

And then she spied a hand waving in front of her face.

"Where did you go?"

"Oh, wool gathering, I guess. What did I miss?"

"I asked you if the alterations were completed on your dress. You know, for my wedding."

"Not yet, but it will be in plenty of time."

Paige grabbed a small notebook from her purse and flipped it open. She made some notes.

"What are you doing?"

"This is my wedding to-do list."

"A handwritten one?"

"Technology isn't my friend, as you know."

"Yes, I do." She craned her neck to see the list. "What else do you have on there?"

"Not too much. I've finished the flowers, dresses. Quinn took the guy's stuff and music." She made a face. He said he had 'the perfect idea.' Goodness knows what he means. We'll see."

"You must really love him if you're trusting him with it."

A dreamy expression washed over her face. "I really do."

Amy swallowed down the sadness threatening to envelope her. "What about the honeymoon?"

"Not sure. I have a few days off after the wedding, before school starts again. We might go away. Then there's spring break. But I'll be pretty pregnant by then. I really don't know. I left it to him as well."

"You can always take a belated one." A short bell sounded, warning them their lunch break was about to end. Amy gathered up her trash. "Guess we have to get back to it."

Paige grinned at her. "You're not fooling anyone. You love being back."

"It's not horrible." She laughed at her friend's outraged expression. "Okay, I love it. I'll see you later."

All the way back to her temporary classroom, Amy thought about her friend's upcoming wedding. Acid swirled in her stomach. She wanted to be thrilled for her Paige and Quinn. And she was. On one level. But the thought of watching them marry, knowing she and Andrew never would, placed a damper on the event.

The noise coming from her class shoved away those gloomy thoughts. She had bigger fish to fry at the moment.

*****

Across town, Mac stretched and yawned. He glanced at his phone and groaned. Two in the afternoon. He'd never mastered the art of sleeping during the day. Rolling over on his back, he stared at the ceiling and wondered about Amy's day. She'd probably finish soon. Did it go okay? Was she exhausted? He flung an arm over his eyes to block the winter sun seeping in through the blinds.

He didn't have the right to wonder about her day. Did he? For so long, their relationship had been more adversarial than anything. No, that wasn't the right word. They hadn't really had a relationship. He was the guy who didn't save the man she loved. He feared Amy would always think of him that way.

But the past few weeks had gone better. They'd run together, shared a few meals. While it wasn't a lot, it had to count for something. Didn't it? *Why did he care?* Now that was the better question. He'd grown up in their little town hating the Windsors. No, not hating. Hate was too strong. Resented them if he was being honest. Everything looked easy for them.

The thought made him sit straight up in bed. Things weren't easy for them because they had money. Amy's loss proved that. Maybe it was time he changed his thinking. Maybe it was years past time.

He jumped out of bed, grinning, and headed for the shower. He had an idea.

Chapter Fifteen

Amy turned on to her block after a very long first day back. She'd turned down Paige's offer for dinner. All she wanted was a glass of wine and a hot bath. Who knew twenty-two second graders could tire her out this much? Luck was on her side as she found a parking spot right in front of the converted Victorian, she once again called home. And then she spotted Mac sitting on her top step. Next to a picnic basket of all things. What was he plotting? A quick thrill ran the length of her spine. She ignored it and opened her car door.

"Hey," he called from the porch. He started toward her. "How was your day, Teach?"

"Long. Exhausting." She grinned. "Fabulous." She gathered her stuff, not bothering to ask why he was here. She never knew with him.

"You're probably wondering why I'm here." He looked down at his jeans and boots. "Clearly not for a run."

"You would have been flying solo. I'm bushed."

He closed the gap between them, sliding her bulging bag from her shoulder. "Let me help." Without waiting for a reply, Mac turned and walked to the door, grabbing the picnic basket on the way.

She watched his long stride, and butt if she was being honest with herself, and grinned. The fatigue slid off her.

"What's in the basket?" she asked, joining him at the front door.

He stood aside while she unlocked it. "Dinner. After today, I figured you'd be tired and hungry. Hungry I can help with."

She turned toward him, very aware of the clean, male scent coming from his body. "I hope you brought enough. I could eat a bear."

He followed her inside, kicking the door closed with his foot. "No bear but enough food. You'll see. Why don't you freshen up? I'll lay out dinner."

She glanced into his eyes. And saw interest there. Not sure how she felt about it, she smiled instead. "I'll be right back."

Amy walked into her bedroom, closing the door and leaning back against it for a moment. *Wow! The man packed a punch.* She straightened up and stripped off her clothes and the day's weariness. Going for comfort, she grabbed a pair of yoga pants and an old hoodie. After all, she wasn't trying to impress Mac. Was she? Shaking her head at the thought, she pulled her hair out of the braid she'd worn all day, running her fingers through it to comb out the length of it.

Before she lost her nerve, she opened her bedroom door and rejoined him in the kitchen.

*****

Mac turned at her entry and sucked in a breath. Wow! Even wearing old sweats, Amy Windsor made quite a sight. He pulled out one chair for her. "Here you go. Take a seat. Dinner is ready."

She brushed by him, inhaling the scent unique to him once again. "Did you get enough sleep?"

He laughed. "Is there ever enough sleep? I don't know how those night shift people do it. There's too much light, and noise, during the day. I could use a few more hours." He stifled a large yawn, as if to prove his point.

"You didn't have to bring me dinner. Again. Although, I appreciate it. All I could picture was a glass of wine and a long, hot bath."

Mac stumbled at the image of her wearing bubbles, and nothing else, almost dropping their dinners. "Uh, well, I can pour you a glass of wine if you want. You're on your own with the bubble bath." He placed a steaming chicken pot pie in front of her and then another across from her.

"Who said anything about bubbles?"

He sat across from her and smiled into her eyes. "In my version, there are bubbles."

Mac enjoyed the light pink wash across her cheeks.

"Oh." She picked up a fork, poking a hole in the top of her pie. Steam and the most delicious aroma escaped. "Is this from The Sunshine Café?" She licked her lips.

"It is. I love her cooking." Being a paramedic, Mac knew you couldn't actually swallow your own tongue. But the sight of her licking her lips in anticipation for dinner made him almost prove it wrong.

"How did you know it's my favorite restaurant in town?" She took a small bite, oohing and aahing at the explosion of tastes on her tongue.

"Lucky guess. Or maybe I texted Paige."

Amy threw back her head and laughed. "Now you've done it. There'll be no rest for me."

He tilted his head.

"Paige seems to think you and I would be a great idea. You furthered her cause."

Mac sat back, placing his fork down. "Would it be the worst idea?" For the life of him, he didn't know which of them he was asking.

"Oh." She looked at him, and the smile slid from her face. "I didn't mean anything by it. It's just, uh, well, you know."

He leaned across the table a bit to be closer to her. "Know what?"

"I, uh, am not really dating right now. That's all."

"Oh, right." He took up his fork and ate a bite of his

dinner. "If you were, uh, dating again, would you go out with me?"

"I would," she answered without any hesitation.

"Okay. Good to know." He took a few more bites, more to keep his hands busy while his heart thundered in his chest. "And this thing you and I are already doing." He waved his fork between them. "What would you consider this? We have meals together. We go running. You've even spent the night at my house."

"All true. Although the last part had more to do with the amount of alcohol you plied me with." She grinned around a heaping forkful of pie.

"I don't remember pouring whisky down your throat."

"True. And you were kind enough to not take advantage of the situation." She ducked her head as she said it.

"Amy, look at me." He waited until she did. "I would never take advantage of the situation with anyone. Least of all you."

She held up a hand. "I'm sorry. Of course, you wouldn't. I was joking. I know you'd never do that."

"Good." He fumbled with his napkin, wiping the corners of his mouth. "I know you don't know me well, but I'd like to think you know I'm not capable of that."

"This conversation is insane. I never thought that. It was stupid to mention it, even in joking. I am truly sorry."

Now he felt like an idiot. "There's no need to apologize. Not sure why I get, uh, stupid around you."

"Maybe it's because you think I'm a princess?" she asked with a smirk.

His turn to feel uncomfortable with the conversation. "I never should have called you that. I was being stupid. I resented you, your family really, all those years. I never thought to realize." He stopped before putting his foot any further into his mouth.

"What didn't you realize about the Windsors, Mac?" There was the slightest touch of steel in her voice.

Man, he'd really done it now. "I never stopped to consider having money and a name people recognize isn't a bullet proof vest. Trouble still finds you."

And the slight bit of color she had drained from her face. She set her napkin down slowly, as though it were made of glass. "No, Mac, having money nor the surname Windsor does not protect you." A harsh laugh ripped from her throat. "It certainly didn't save me." She stood, her chest heaving with the effort to breathe. "Maybe I had too much, Mac. Did you ever consider that? I have. Maybe I was too lucky. Too rich. Too spoiled. And Andrew paid the price."

She turned her back to him. He watched her take a few deep breaths before she whirled around again. "It's the part you don't get, Mac. I would give up everything I have. The name. The money. Everything, if I could have Andrew back again, even for a day." She dropped her eyes to the floor. "But the Windsor name can't conjure magic," she finished on a whisper.

He stood up, not sure what to do. He'd hurt her without meaning to. And he didn't know how to fix it. He stood next to her, gathering her in his arms. Her body stood rigid within his embrace. "I never meant to hurt you, Amy," he whispered into her hair. He bestowed a quick kiss on her forehead before walking out into the cold evening.

*****

Amy stood there, long after he was gone, not moving. She'd forgotten this level of pain. The one where she swore her heart would shatter into tiny pieces. She wasn't a stupid person. She knew what some people thought of her. Of her family. She didn't realize Mac numbered amongst them.

Exhausted, she fled into the bathroom and started a hot bath. After adding a liberal amount of bubbles (he was right, damn him), she stripped and slid into the water. Amy leaned back, resting her head against a towel and closed her eyes, willing the water to wash away her troubles. Her grief. Her loneliness. It was a lot to ask of a hot bath.

She'd overreacted. To Mac. Again. What was it about him that brought out the worst in her? She slid lower, until only her nose and up remained out of the water. She didn't care what some paramedic thought anyway. *Great! Now she sounded like Alex.* And the bigger problem was she did.

Mac being a paramedic had nothing to do with it. Andrew had been a firefighter. Career choice and income level never mattered to her. A kind heart. A sense of humor. These things mattered. Mac was a decent man. She may not know him well, but she knew these things about him. Besides, he and Quinn had been friends for years. Paige's fiancé made a great barometer when it came to people.

No, she had to apologize to him. Again. Great! If she were more like her mother, she'd bake him a cake and call it a day. But any cake made by her would only add insult to injury. No, she'd have to put on her big girl panties and apologize.

She sat until the water chilled before getting out and jumping in the shower. After a quick rinse and washing her hair, she got out and put on her oldest, ugliest flannel PJs. They might be tattered and a disgrace, according to her mother, but she loved them. They were the comfort food of pajamas.

After pouring herself a long overdue glass of wine, Amy padded out to the living room and pulled a folder from her shoulder bag. She'd asked the kids to write a few sentences about themselves. Something to give her a better idea about them for the next few days. She plopped down on the couch to read them. Most talked about their families, pets, and what they liked to do.

Then she picked up Danny's. And her heart broke.

"My name is Danny. I used to have a little sister. She drowned. My mom is sad now. My dad yells a lot."

She grabbed her phone and hit the preset for Paige. It went to voicemail before she remembered her "date" with Quinn. She hung up without leaving a message and took a sip of her wine. The poor boy. No wonder he acted out.

Next, she chose Adam, the little boy Danny picked on

today.

"I used to live far away. Now I live here. I don't know many people. I like to play soccer. I miss my friends."

Also sad but for a very different reason. She wasn't sure how long Adam had lived in Windsor Falls. Maybe she could talk to his parents about signing him up for soccer when the weather improved. Maybe she could talk to the gym teacher about it.

A knock at the door broke her train of thought. She grabbed her glass and got up to answer it. "You could have called me back, Paige," she said as she pulled open the door.

"First your mother and now Paige. Is it my cologne?"

"Oh." She stepped back, allowing him room to enter. "No, you smell nice. Very manly. Not at all like a woman." And wanted to smack her head against the wall. Even more so when she saw his grin.

"Manly, huh? Is that a good thing? Not like a gym or old socks…"

"Really? Now you're fishing." She closed the door and took a breath. "But, now that you're back, let me apologize." He started to stop her, but she pushed through. "No, really. I overreacted. A lot. And I am sorry." She twisted the silver ring on her thumb. "I didn't feel anything for a long time. Now, I feel too much."

"While I appreciate it, I came back to apologize to you. I didn't mean what I said. Not really. Maybe a long time ago, I thought that way." He looked down at his shoes. "When I was growing up. You have to know I'd never wish anything bad for you." He stepped forward, pushing some hair behind her ear. "I want you to be happy, Amy. You deserve it. You deserve all good things."

"Come on in." She led the way to the couch, flipping on the gas fireplace before sinking into the plush cushions, and took a sip of wine. "Would you like a glass?"

"No thanks. Not much of a wine drinker." He sat at the opposite end of the couch and turned to face her. "Love your pajamas. Very sexy."

She threw a pillow at him, hitting him square in the chest. "I will have you know I dress for comfort." She pointed to her flannel top. "And this is very comfortable. And warm. These nights are ridiculously chilly."

"Maybe you should get a dog to sleep with. They'd keep you warm."

"Funny you should mention it. I've been thinking I need a pet. Living alone gets, uh, lonely." *God, could she sound anymore pathetic?*

"Sam knows a lot about rescues. And Brendan. Maybe you should talk to them."

"I will. When the time is right. I've only been back here for about a second. And then there's the wedding. I have to get through that first." She thought about how it sounded. "What I mean is..."

Mac held up a hand. "I get it. You're very happy for them, after all she is your best friend. But this can't be easy for you."

She pulled an old afghan across her to fend against the chill threatening to consume her. "Yes, that's it exactly. I am happy for Paige and Quinn. Of course, I am. But it doesn't mean it's not also painful for me." She took a big gulp of her wine. "Don't worry, I'm limiting myself to one glass tonight."

"Hey, whatever works. And you are in your own home."

"Yep. As happy as I am for them, I'm also dreading it. I know this makes me a terrible person. And I'd never tell Paige."

"It makes you human, Amy. That's all." He scooted a little closer, grabbing her free hand. "I'll help you anyway I can. If you need to yell at me, or even punch me, I'm there for you."

She placed her mostly empty glass on the coffee table and took both of his hands in hers. "Despite what you think, you are truly kind and nice." She squeezed his hands as he groaned. "And those are two good qualities to have." She pulled one hand free and covered a yawn.

"And boring as well," he quipped.

"No, not at all. I didn't sleep very well last night."

"Nervous about the first day?"

"Yes, that, too."

He cocked his head, looking into her eyes. "What else kept you up?"

She wanted to look away but couldn't make herself do it. He stared so intently, she felt he could see all the way into her soul. "I miss him," she said on a sigh. "The bed felt too big. Too empty."

"Maybe I could help."

Chapter Sixteen

Mac wished the words back before they even left his mouth. But it was too late. He's said them. And she'd heard them. And pulled back from him, as if she needed more distance between them. And then she pulled the rug out from under him.

"Okay."

His heart executed a painful little somersault in his chest. "Okay?" Maybe he hadn't heard her right.

She stood. Bolted really. "Never mind," she muttered and took her glass to the kitchen. He watched her rinse and place it in the dishwasher, suspecting she needed to keep busy. And her back to him. But he wasn't letting her off so easy.

"I meant it, Amy. Why don't we just go to sleep? You won't feel lonely in the house."

"I, uh, okay." She stopped talking as if afraid of what she might say next.

"Okay then. One thing, though. And it's kind of a deal breaker."

Her eyes grew wide. She twisted the dish towel in her hand. "Yes?"

"Do you snore?"

And then she burst out laughing. "That's your deal breaker?" she asked when she had finally stopped laughing.

"Yes, I'm afraid it is. I had a girlfriend once who snored like a truck driver. Killed the relationship." He could feel the corners of his mouth lifting in a smile. He'd say anything, do anything, if he could make her laugh like that again.

"Good to know. Well, I don't snore. At least I've never been told I do." She took her time folding the dishtowel over the oven handle. "Ah, let me grab you a toothbrush. I think I have an extra." She bolted toward her bedroom as though demons chased her.

Mac stood in her tiny kitchen, watching until she disappeared from sight. What had he gotten himself into? He'd agreed to sleep, just sleep, with the most beautiful woman he'd ever met. No way this could end in disaster. He was still shaking his head when she appeared again.

"Here you go." She held out a toothbrush, still in its packaging. "You can use the master bathroom. There's toothpaste on the counter. Oh, and a fresh towel on the rack."

"Thanks," he murmured before heading into her bedroom. It looked different now. All traces of Andrew were gone, and some of her personal times had appeared. He removed his boots and continued into the bathroom. The room smelled of her. And her recent bath. A slightly floral scent hung in the air. He liked it. It had been a long time since he'd been in such close proximity with a woman. Too long.

He brushed his teeth and then stared at himself in the mirror. *This is Amy, and you guys are friends. Remember, she isn't ready for anything else.* Done with his pep talk, Mac left the bathroom. She stood at one side of the bed. The look on her face screamed discomfort.

"This is the side I usually sleep on."

"Doesn't matter to me. I could sleep anywhere. Never have trouble sleeping." He hoped it remained true tonight.

"Good. Do you need anything else?"

"No, I'm good. Gonna take off some of these layers if it's all right by you."

"Oh, of course. I didn't think about it. I, uh, don't have anything that might fit."

He laughed, hoping to break the tension. "I sure hope not."

"Well, okay then." She crossed the room, turning out the overhead light, plunging most of the room into darkness. Only the weak light from her bedside lamp remained.

Mac waited until she crawled into bed, her back turned to him, before shucking off most of his clothing. In deference to the situation, he left on his boxer briefs.

She clicked off the lamp as he slid beneath the downed comforter. Only pale moonlight filtering in from behind her curtains remained. He liked a cool, dark room for sleeping. Mac lay on his back, very aware of the warm, beautiful female mere inches from him. And the tension radiating off her in waves.

Gritting his teeth, he pulled a startled Amy into his arms. "This won't work if you can't relax," he muttered into her ear. She remained stiff as a board, then muscle by muscle began to relax against his chest.

"Sorry. It's been awhile."

"No worries. Been awhile for me, too." He held her in the dark, listening to her breathing as it slowed and evened out. "Tell me what kind of dog you want."

A short giggle met his ears. "Nice segue. I hadn't really given it much thought. Something furry and soft who will greet me at the door as if I'd been to war."

Laughter rumbled from his chest. "Nice. I wouldn't mind having one either."

"Why don't you have a dog?"

"Doesn't seem fair with the hours I work. Wouldn't want the little fella to be home alone so much. Someday, though. I definitely want a dog when I have kids."

"Oh. You want kids?"

"Yes, and don't sound surprised. I think I'd make a pretty good dad."

"No, it's not that. And I think you would, too."

"Then what is it?"

"I'm not sure. I've never really thought of you as a family

man." She sighed, and he felt it through to his toes. "I said it wrong. I've never seen you with someone, you know like a girlfriend. I guess I thought you were like Quinn. Before he met Paige anyway."

"You mean a confirmed bachelor?"

"Yes."

"Not at all. Quinn was afraid of committing after losing his dad on the job. I never worried about it. I haven't met the right person. And it's important to me. My parents had a very short, very bad marriage. I don't want that. I want to marry once, grow old together. I guess it makes me old-fashioned."

"Call it what you will, but it sounds nice. My parents are still married, going on forty years. I want that. Wanted that. I thought I had that."

He strained to hear the last part; her voice had grown so faint. Mac gathered her closer in his arms. "You can still have the whole package, Amy. A.J. dying like he did isn't fair. It sucks, but, you're still young. You have your whole life ahead of you."

"I know. But sometimes I feel ninety. And I'm not sure I could risk the pain again. Losing him almost killed me."

"More than anything, A.J. loved you. He'd want you to be happy."

"I know. I want it too."

"Look how far you've come in a few short weeks. Don't pressure yourself. Give yourself time to heal and move on with your life. You'll meet someone."

"Maybe."

They lay in the dark, each alone with their thoughts. He wondered if he'd already met the right one. If maybe he held her in his arms right now. But how to convince her? How to convince himself?

"Thank you, Mac," she murmured in a voice thick with sleep.

He kissed her soft hair at the crown of her head. "You're welcome." He didn't know if she heard. Her breathing had deepened. He stayed where he was, Amy lying within the circle of his arms, and thought about the past few days. They weren't fighting as much. And they'd spent a lot of time together. But she wasn't over A.J., and he wasn't willing to be anyone's second choice.

*****

Amy awoke slowly, the heat from Andrew's body next to her chasing away the predawn chill permeating the room. She snuggled closer, molding herself against him and sighed. She'd missed this for so long. Then her eyes popped open. Andrew was dead, not next to her.

She glanced at the man sleeping at her side. Mac, the very real, flesh and blood, man lay on his stomach, one arm thrown over the opposite side. Not Andrew. Silently, she turned away from him, clenching her body into the smallest ball she could create. For a moment, really the length of a single heartbeat, she'd thought Andrew was with her. She buried her face in her hands while regret stabbed through her. Heaviness settled in her chest while the reality of the situation hit home. Andrew would never lie beside her again. She knew it. Had known it for eighteen months. And yet, somehow, she'd forgotten. She slowed her breathing, loathe to wake him. She needed to gain control before she could face him.

"I can hear you thinking all the way over here," he mumbled in a sleepy, delicious tone.

She lay there, stiff as a board, and refused to answer him. Maybe he'd think she was still asleep. Maybe he'd leave. But then she felt his hand on her shoulder.

"Amy, what's wrong? I know you're awake."

How to tell him she'd awoken, thinking he was her dead fiancé? "Nothing," she muttered, taking the coward's way out.

The mattress moved as he shifted his body. His warm breath touched her shoulder. One hand brushed hair out of her face. "Did you sleep okay?"

"Yes, thanks. Did you?" She hated her formal tone but couldn't help it. Surely, he would need to leave for work. She could get through this for a few minutes.

"I'm not leaving until you tell me." He yawned. "There's no reason to be embarrassed."

He thought she was embarrassed to awaken next to him. "You're in my bed because I begged you to stay last night. Nothing embarrassing there."

"You didn't beg. And nothing happened. I'm even happy to report you don't snore after all."

She knew nothing had happened. She just didn't know if she was happy about it or sad. "I did. I know, and I told you so."

And he laughed. "Honestly, Amy, a beautiful woman asked me to stay. Much worse things have happened to me."

"I'll bet no one has ever asked you to stay to sleep. Not, uh, you know."

"Sex, Amy. You can say the word. And for the record, I'm all for sex. With you in fact, but you're not ready for it. And I stayed because you asked me to, not begged me to. And I slept very well." He glanced at his phone on the side table. "But now I have to go. And not because I don't want to stay but because I have a shift in a little over an hour." And with that as her warning, he got out of bed, picked up his discarded clothing, and walked into her bathroom. Wearing only his underwear. And she watched him until he closed the door, then pulled a pillow over her face.

She remembered the moments of inane conversation they'd shared before she fell asleep. She'd missed it. Missed the closeness of another person next to her. A presence in the dark. Did it matter if it was Mac, or any other random guy? Maybe.

"Still thinking way too hard I see."

He'd come back into the room without her hearing. She removed the pillow from her face. "Guilty. And now it's my turn to start my day." She got up and made the bed. Anything to keep busy until he left. Until she could think clearly again.

But he moved to the other side, his side, and tucked the comforter under the pillows. Damn him.

"Need anything else before I leave?"

She pasted on an overly bright smile. "No, I'm good. Uh, thanks." She turned to escape into the bathroom, but he caught her by the arm, hauling her against him. And kissed her thoroughly.

"In case you're wondering, I've wanted to do this since I walked in last night." He hugged her then let go, walking out of the room.

She waited until she heard the outer door close before letting out the breath she didn't know she held. Her fingers moved of their own accord, touching the lips he'd kissed. She couldn't stop the grin if she wanted to. To avoid thinking too long about it, she headed into the shower.

After grabbing a quick breakfast, Amy headed out to face the second graders again.

Chapter Seventeen

Mac whistled a tune as he pushed himself in the station's weight room. His shift had ended over an hour ago, and he had only a few reps left before he collapsed. He heard the door open and close but paid no attention to it. Until Quinn appeared over his face, grinning.

He placed the bar on the holders and grabbed a towel to wipe the sweat from his eyes. "I'd get up, but I don't think I can."

"Push it a bit too far, did you?"

He shrugged. "Maybe. What brings you by?"

"It's Friday."

"Very good. You've learned the days of the week."

"Ha, very funny. It's Friday, and we need to pick out tuxedos before Paige kills both of us."

"Oh, right." He rolled his eyes. "Someone's whipped."

Instead of fighting back, his friend grinned. "Yep. Freely admitted and wouldn't change it for the world."

He felt a funny little pain around his heart he doubted came from weightlifting. "Give me a few minutes to shower and change."

"I'll wait."

He made his way to the locker room and turned on the shower as hot as he could get it. The pipes in this building were finicky at best. He either froze or scalded himself. He took a very brief, and chilly, shower before pulling on his after work usual choice. Jeans and a hoody. He headed out to find Quinn.

"Twenty-two minutes. Not bad."

"I would have taken longer, but I didn't feel like freezing off a piece of my anatomy I've grown to love."

His friend laughed and patted him on the back. "Let's go before the place closes."

"Does Paige give you your balls back every evening?"

"Funny. Let's go." He led the way to his truck, and Mac followed him. No sense in taking two cars.

"Has Paige mentioned Amy this week?"

"No why?"

"Just curious. She taught this week." And he waited for the inevitable comment. He didn't have to wait long.

"I hear you and Amy have been hanging out. What's up? I thought she hated you."

"She never hated me."

"She wasn't your biggest fan either. And as far as I can remember, you've not been a fan of the Windsors."

"We're friends, okay? What's with the inquisition?"

"I asked a question." He took his eyes off the road to stare at Mac for a moment. "What's with you?"

He ran a hand through his short hair. "I don't know what I'm doing."

"Then you're probably not doing it right," he joked.

"I'm not kidding."

"Oh. Sorry. Tell me."

"I've been spending time with Amy. At first, we ran in the mornings. I wanted to help her out."

"And then?"

"That's it. I don't know. I think about her when I'm not with her. She's going through so much right now, trying to get her life back on track and all."

"Sounds like you like her. Not to sound like middle school."

"Too late, but I do. I mean who wouldn't? She's beautiful and funny. But she's not at the same place I am right now. Not sure she ever will be."

"You mean about A.J."

"Yes."

"I don't know what to say. It was a tough loss. For all of us. But she loved him. And he loved her, a lot. It was a mutual thing, from the very first moment."

"Yeah."

"What are you thinking?"

Mac shook his head, laughing more at himself than anything. "I have no idea. I enjoy being with her. We talk. We share a meal. And it's great. But the chemistry? Wow! Blows my socks off."

Quinn pulled into the parking lot of the formal wear store. He didn't answer until he turned off the car and turned in his seat. "Are you saying you've slept with her?"

"No! But would it be a problem if I did?"

"Ah, yeah. She's Paige's best friend. As in from conception. You know this. When something goes wrong, it would be a disaster."

"Why does something have to go wrong?" He wished he had an answer.

"I don't know it will, Mac. But she's, uh, fragile right now. She's starting to live again after losing her fiancé. It might be too much."

"Not to mention the fact that she isn't over A.J."

"Yep."

"Whatever. Obviously, getting involved on any level with her is a mistake."

"I didn't say that. Be careful. Tread lightly."

"That's just it. I don't want to." He clapped a hand on his friend's shoulder. "Let's go get you looking decent for your wedding."

*****

"He spent the night?" Paige clapped a hand over her mouth. "Sorry."

"Gee, maybe someone in Virginia or South Carolina didn't hear you." She grabbed a fry from Paige's plate.

"I am sorry, but wow. I mean really, wow! I never saw it coming."

"Nothing happened." She almost laughed aloud at the way her friend's smile died. "We slept together, as in went to sleep."

"In the same bed?"

"Yes, that's what together means."

"Wow again. You have a lot of self-control. Not sure I could sleep next to him and not, uh, you know."

"Paige!"

She rubbed her belly. "Can't help it. These hormones have me all over the place. And, damn, the man is fine."

Luckily, she had swallowed her soda, or she might have sprayed it across the table. "Since when do you curse?" Her friend was forever saying things like shish kebob to avoid cursing. She feared she would slip in front of her young students.

"Since my brain has been awash in pregnancy hormones." She grinned, the sweet smile she expected from Paige. "And I love it. I blame all kinds of bad behavior on this little nugget." To prove a point, she grabbed a fry and popped it in her mouth. "See? Six weeks ago, I would have worried about the calories."

"I thought 'eating for two' meant making healthier choices. Not to burst your bubble."

"Oh, it does. I am very aware of everything I eat. I'm not sweating the calories as much."

"Ah. Sounds like a plan."

"Nice try. Back to Mac. Tell me everything."

Because Paige was her oldest friend and favorite person on the planet, she did. And didn't know what to do when tears coursed down her friend's face. "What's wrong?" She handed her some napkins.

Paige grabbed them, waving them in the air first. "I told you he's the nicest guy ever." The last bit came out on a wail as she swabbed her face.

The word nice brought laughter bubbling out of Amy. "He hates it when I call him nice. Or kind for that matter. Acted like I ran over his puppy."

"Amy, you didn't! It's one thing for me to call him nice. He's not into me. And I didn't say it to his face. Men don't want to be thought of nice or kind. 'Nice guys finish last' and all that. I'm sure he'd rather be thought of as handsome or sexy. Both of which he is, by the way."

"Yes, you've said. Several times. Should Quinn be worried?" she joked.

"Of course not. He knows he is the only one for me."

The sentence set her back. "What if there's only one? For everyone? I loved Andrew with every fiber of my being. And he died."

"Amy, honey, I know you did. And he loved you as much. But, you're right, he isn't here anymore. He wouldn't want you mourning him for the rest of your life. You're not even thirty. Are you supposed to be alone forever?"

"No, and I know he wouldn't want this for me. As I wouldn't have wanted it for him. But how do I know the next man won't die? Won't leave me?" She dropped her eyes to the tabletop. "I don't think I could survive it again."

She heard Paige get up. Next thing she knew, Paige landed in the chair next to her, arms wrapped around her. "There aren't any guarantees in life, Amy. You and I know more than most, sadly. You know Quinn struggled with ever getting involved after losing his father so young."

"I know. Mac and I talked about it. I know the odds are in my favor. But the thought." She stopped and tried to swallow the large lump in her throat. "The thought of surviving the loss again." She shook her head.

"You don't have to make any decisions today. Go with it. Have fun. It's not like he asked you to marry him." She winced. "Oh, Amy, I'm sorry."

"It's fine. I don't want you walking on eggshells around me anymore."

Paige picked up her own soda, tapping it against Amy's. "A toast. To my friend and her starting over." She leaned in. "And hopefully having sex with the second hottest man in Windsor Falls. And I'm going to need details."

Amy took a drink, shaking her head at her outrageous friend. She couldn't, however, deny the tiny shocks racing through her body at the thought.

Chapter Eighteen

Amy stood on Mac's porch, raising her hand to knock before she lost her nerve. This might be the most impulsive thing she'd ever done. She knocked twice.

"Hey." Mac stood in the door, wearing old, worn grey sweats and a T-shirt. And looking as delicious as any dessert her friend Kat had ever created.

Taking a deep breath, Amy entered without asking, shutting the door behind her. She placed her hands on either side of his face, the five-o-clock shadow tickling her palms, and kissed him. For a moment, she felt his surprise in the stiffness of his muscles. And then he melted. Or maybe she did. All rational thought disappeared. She slid her fingers into his short hair, pulling him closer until no space existed between them.

In one swift movement, he flipped their positions, pinning her against the door with his body. The kiss went on. And on. Desire raced along her nerves, heated her blood. She moaned into his mouth. Or maybe he did. She couldn't get enough of him. Amy dropped her hands to his chest, molding the muscles she found beneath the shirt he wore. Frustrated at even a thin layer between him and her searching fingers, she slid both hands under the edge of the T-shirt. Warm, hard flesh delighted her.

And then he broke the kiss, took a step back, and dragged in air. "I know I'm going to regret asking, but what was that?"

She cursed the heat burning her cheeks. "I don't want to be alone tonight. But even more, I want to be with you." She sighed. "I want you." She stepped around him, removing her coat and throwing it over the back of the sofa. Without stopping, she approached the door, kicking off her shoes. Finally, she turned to face him. "What do you think?"

"I think I'm a very lucky man." And that was all he said before sweeping her up in his arms and all but running to his bedroom. Once inside, he shut the door before turning to her. "Are you sure, Amy?"

"I was when I got here. If you keep asking me, I might not be."

"Tell me what's going on." He sat on the bed, patting the spot next to him. "Talk to me."

She crossed the room, wiping her palms on her jean-clad thighs. She sank onto the bed, turning to face him. "I don't know what this is." She waved a hand back and forth. "Between us, I mean. But I like you. And I'm attracted to you. I feel, uh, things. Things I haven't felt in a very long time. Is it enough for you?"

He leaned in, closing the small space between them. "Say my name."

She tilted her head. "What? I don't understand, Mac."

He kissed her forehead, his lips making their way to her mouth. After a moment, he broke the light kiss. "There. You said my name. I needed you to know who you're with."

"You're not Andrew. I am aware. You're Mac, the very nice and kind." She stopped, laughing at his wince. "And sexy man. More than anything, right now I want to have sex with you."

"That's all I needed to hear." He sealed his words with a deep, lingering kiss.

And the heat exploded between them. All the pent-up frustration and lust, building over days, exploded. She clawed at his T-shirt, desperate to remove the barrier.

"Let me help you," he growled. And the offending garment flew through the air.

Amy sat back, staring at his broad chest and sculpted abdomen like a starving person before a buffet. What to touch first? Where to taste first? She leaned in, running her tongue from his navel, upward and across his chest, ending in the spot behind one ear. She nibbled there for a moment, while he moved on the bed.

"Like it, do you?" she whispered into his ear.

"Let me show you how much." He pushed her back onto the bed and grabbed both of her wrists, trapping her with his hips.

She arched one brow. "That much, huh?" The weight of his erection pressed into her belly. She slid one hand free from his grasp. Slowly, taking her time, her fingers creeped down his taut abdomen and under the loose waistband of his sweats until she grasped him in her hand. The low, guttural noise coming from him pleased her.

"I think someone in this room is overdressed." Mac unbuttoned her flannel shirt, one button at a time, kissing the skin he exposed as he went. When he finished, he pushed the material off both arms, leaving her in only a cotton camisole. She could feel her nipples peak under his gaze. Then his mouth captured one, sucking it in until she thought she would explode. "Please," she begged him.

"Please what? I need you to tell me."

She opened her eyes, looking straight into his darkened gaze. "I need you, Mac. All of you. I need you inside me. Now."

"Your wish is my command." He pulled her hand from his sweatpants then unbuttoned her jeans.

She laid back on the bed, arching her back to allow him better access. In the next moment, her jeans joined his sweats on the floor. But she didn't have time to feel the chill in the room. His hard, hot body covered hers, the length of him glued to her. His mouth fitted to hers. His tongue traced the line of her lips, seeking entrance. She swirled her tongue to his, twisting and dancing together.

She couldn't get enough of him. Her hands roamed across his broad back, tracing each muscle and sinew she discovered. He did the same with her, running his hands down her sides and across her lower abdomen. She tensed for a moment when he traced a finger under the band of her panties.

This brought his head up. Stilled his fingers. "Are you okay?"

The gentle tone of his voice touched her bounding heart, calming it. "I'm fine. Just a bit rusty." She buried her face in his bare shoulder. "I don't want to disappoint you."

"Hey, look at me." He didn't speak again until she lifted her head. "I'm here, with you. Exactly where I want to be. Nothing you do could disappoint me." He leaned forward, kissing her very lightly on the lips. "I want this to be good for you. Tell me what you want. Show me."

She took his hand, placing it on her breast. "I want to feel you, Mac. Everywhere."

He grinned. "That I can do." Taking her peak between his fingers, he teased until the line between pleasure and pain blurred. Tension built low in her belly, spreading warmth in all directions. When she thought she couldn't take it anymore, he replaced his fingers with his tongue, teasing the peaked flesh, pulling it into his mouth and nipping gently.

"Oh," she cried into his neck. She took his ear lobe in her mouth, biting down enough to get a reaction. The sensation of him moaning around her nipple raised her hips off the bed. "Please. Now."

He straightened and grabbed her camisole from the bottom, pulling it over her head. Then he laid her flat on her back in the middle of the bed. Reaching into the bedside drawer, Mac removed a foil packet.

She took it from his hands. "Here, let me." Amy raised up on one elbow. After tearing open the packet, she rolled the condom down the length of him. Slowly. Carefully. Taking her time. She smiled at the quivering of his muscles.

"Play time is over." He pushed her down once again,

easing between her legs.

She opened them, lifting her knees in welcome. "You're too far away," she complained. Reaching up, Amy grabbed him by the shoulders, bringing him down until their bodies touched.

He slid a hand under her panties. She didn't flinch this time, merely wiggled her hips in encouragement. He drew them down and off her, one finger finding her center. The electric shocks spread from her core all the way through her body. She panted as his finger explored deeper.

She tossed her head back and forth, hair going everywhere. "Yes, Mac, right there. Please, I need you now."

It was all the encouragement he needed, because he withdrew his finger and pressed the tip of his penis to her opening. "Are you sure?" he asked.

She opened her eyes, staring right at him. "I have never been surer. Please."

He didn't ask anything else, but slid into her, inch by inch, until she felt the length of him buried in her. For a moment, they stayed still. No one moved. No one spoke. Then he moved his hips, setting a pace which took her spiraling upwards. She met his hips, stroke for stroke, clenching around him until he groaned aloud.

Mac lowered his head, taking one turgid nipple in his mouth. It was too much. She closed her eyes and flew apart into thousands of tiny pieces. "Oh my," she purred. Amy opened her eyes to see his face tighten. She squeezed her muscles around him one more time to finish him off.

His back arched for a long moment before he collapsed on top of her. She kissed his shoulder, reveling in the salty taste of his sweat. *She'd done that.*

He rolled to his side, taking her with him in his embrace. "Wow! I don't have any other words for it."

She grinned at him. "I know a few. How about stupendous? Terrific? Mind-blowing?" Anything else she might have said, he cut off with a kiss.

"Any of those will do," he quipped when he rose for air.

"I'll be right back."

She watched him rise and walk to the bathroom, seemingly very comfortable in his own skin. She used to feel that way. Glancing down at her nude body, she grimaced. Twenty or so pounds ago, she loved her body. Now, her skinniness taunted her. Her lithe, athletic shape had melded into something closer to starvation victim in her grief. In the dark days, as she thought of them, hours and sometimes days passed without memory of eating. If not for Paige, she might have wasted away. The thought shamed her. How self-indulgent her grief had been. Surely, most didn't have the luxury. Spouses lost their other halves and went on. Parents lost children but fought through it for the sake of their remaining ones. She didn't have anyone to fight for. And hadn't cared enough about herself to do it. She closed her eyes.

*****

Mac couldn't stop the silly grin on his face. Nor did he care to. When he awoke this morning, he never could have dreamed he'd find himself here, naked, with Amy lying in his bed. He wasn't sure what had come over her since their platonic sleepover the other night, but he wasn't a stupid man. He wouldn't question his luck. He finished cleaning himself up and left the bathroom, whistling a tune to himself.

Amy lay on her side, facing away from him, covers pulled to her chin. He slid in behind her. "Cold already without me?" He leaned over to kiss her, but the stark expression on her face stopped him. His heart sank in his chest. He pushed aside the waterfall of blonde hair hiding her face. "Tell me." Then held his breath. *Please let it be anything but regret. Please don't let her wish he was another man.*

"You'll think me sillier than you already do."

Her tone didn't invite further comment. But he didn't let it stop him. This was too important. She was too important. "I don't think you're silly. Maybe, before I knew you. But not now." He leaned down, hugging her to him. "Please, Amy, tell me."

She rolled all the way over until she faced him, eyes wide. "I wasted a lot of time feeling sorry for myself. Hating the universe for taking him from me." She closed her eyes and blew out a long breath before opening them again. "I'm only now understanding how very selfish I've been. It's not a good feeling."

"Oh, honey. You had a terrible loss. And I don't understand the depth of your pain, but I think you did the only thing you could do. To survive."

"Eighteen months, Mac. I wallowed in my grief, and pity, because that's what it became. A huge, stupid pity party. Yes, I lost the love of my life. Yes, it hurt so badly I couldn't breathe in the beginning. But I'm far from the only person to have suffered a loss. What about Elizabeth? She lost her husband and unborn baby in a matter of days. And she became an ER doctor. And Quinn? He lost his father when he was still a child. He found the courage to love again. To take the chance again. What have I done?"

He wished she would cry. In his head, Amy crying would be the final end to a very sad chapter. And ends meant a new beginning. But she didn't. Her eyes held no expression at all. The bleakness sent cold shivers down his spine.

He slid under the comforter and gathered her in his arms, tucking her head under his chin. "I want you to listen to me. Yes, Elizabeth and Quinn suffered losses. As did Charlie and Brendan. And many other people we know. And yes, they moved on. Did something with their lives. And you will, too. No one can put a timeline on your grief. Not even you. This is your grief. So what if you withdrew into yourself? You did what you had to do to survive the pain."

"But, Mac, it was self-indulgent."

"Did you hurt anyone?"

"I hurt Paige. And what about my family? They must have been so worried about me."

"They're all adults, Amy. They survived. And everyone is

thrilled to have you back. You have to let this go. Wash your hands of it. Turn the corner. Whatever it takes to move on. You have to cut yourself some slack."

"I never considered how much this affected them. I couldn't. I couldn't see past my own pain." Her voice hitched on the last word.

He gathered her closer, willing positive energy into her. "Think about how far you've come in the past two weeks. You're back in your home. You've even gone back to teaching. It counts, Amy. Those are big steps."

"I guess," she whispered. Her breath tickled the hair on his chest, strengthening the connection between them.

"No guessing allowed. Those are important things you've done. Be proud of yourself." He wanted to point out her being in his bed counted for something, too. Something huge in his eyes. But he didn't want to scare her away.

"You're right. I need to look forward, not back." She stretched up and placed a kiss on his cheek. "Do you mind if I stay for a little while longer?" She didn't quite smother a yawn.

"Mind? Try to leave anytime soon." He placed a loud, smacking kiss on her forehead before turning out the light at the bedside. "Close your eyes. I've got you." And he did.

Long after she stilled and her breathing evened out, he lay there in the darkness. Holding her. He didn't want to let her go. Ever. And the thought sent a little thrill through his heart. Followed by terror. She wasn't ready to think about forever with someone other than A.J. She might never be. Only time would tell.

He brushed a hair from her eyes, watching her smooth, even features. Amy Windsor was a beautiful woman, both inside and out. She was the total package: brains, beauty, kindness, intelligence. And wealth. And something cold and heavy settled in his gut. He wasn't from her world. Where summers were spent at the club, playing golf and tennis. Would it matter to her when she woke up and thought about it?

He tried to tamp down the growing feeling of panic. But old lessons died hard. If ever. He grew up wearing hand-me-downs from other families in town. His parents didn't carry fancy names and degrees from big universities. His father was a drunk. And a mean one. Dying from complications of liver disease was the kindest thing he'd ever done for Mac. And who knew about his mother? He hadn't seen her, or even thought about her, in a long time.

If not for his grandmother, who loved him enough for both of his errant parents, and ruled with an iron fist, God knows what would have become of him. She'd been there for him until the day she died. She fed him, gave him a home, and taught him to believe in himself. She watched him struggle through high school, never quite fitting in. She cheered when he got accepted to college, telling him she always knew he'd make something of himself. If only she'd lived long enough to see him graduate with a degree in emergency management. But a lifetime of smoking had taken its toll. Lung cancer had crept up on her, not showing its ugly face until it was too late to do anything about it. He buried her a month after she received the devastating diagnosis.

He still missed her. She was the one person in his life who loved him enough to support him and to call him on his bullshit. Now, it was up to him. He'd earned his paramedic license to give back to his community. Mac loved what he did, although some days were tougher than others.

Amy stirred in his arms, whispered his name. A huge smile broke out on his face. She'd said his name in her sleep. His name! Maybe she dreamed of him. He didn't want her to forget A.J. The man had been like a brother to him. He missed him, too. But Mac needed Amy to make room in her heart for him. He hoped this was a huge first step.

Chapter Nineteen

The next two weeks passed in a blur. Amy extended her stint with the second graders when their regular teacher developed complications from surgery. It would be another few weeks of intensive physical therapy before she could return to the classroom. Although she was sorry to hear it, Amy rejoiced in the opportunity. Her days stayed busy with her young charges. They tired her out most days causing her to limp home exhausted.

But not too tired to grab dinner with Mac. Or breakfast. Or a sleepover. His presence in her life became another unexpected joy. He'd gone from the man she couldn't bear to face to, well, something different. She loathed to put a name on what developed between them. Things flowed nicely, and she wasn't going to be the one to muck it up. No, better to enjoy the time they spent together.

The day of Paige's wedding sped toward them like a freight train. The morning of Christmas Eve found her in town, trying to find last minute gifts for everyone. A light snow fell from the sky, turning Windsor Falls into a magical Christmas card. Storefronts competed for 'best decorated.' The huge tree next to the town square gazebo glowed with thousands of lights.

She ducked into Between the Covers. Jamie greeted her.

"Hey, you! Merry Christmas!"

Amy rushed forward and hugged her friend. "And Merry Christmas to you as well. Enjoying the last-minute rush?"

"You know it. God bless those people who wait. And have the good sense to know books make an excellent gift. You included; I take it."

"Yep, guilty. I thought I'd pick up some pregnancy books for Paige. Show her how excited I am for her."

Jamie threw her arms around Amy. "You're a good egg." She stepped back, taking a long look at her. "How are you, really?"

Sometimes, the question bugged her. But never from her friends. "I'm okay. Taking it day by day. Honestly, I've been too busy to think about it."

"Great. I hear Mac has been responsible for part of your newfound busyness."

"What?"

Jamie's smile dimmed. "Oh, I'm sorry. I thought it was common knowledge."

"Mac and I are friends. That's all." She mentally crossed her fingers. She didn't want to lie to her friend, but she wasn't ready to talk about her and Mac. She hadn't even told Amy she was sleeping with him, a fact which weighed heavily on her mind.

"I'm sorry. I must have misunderstood. You know how Windsor Falls is sometimes."

"No, I'm sorry. I shouldn't snap off your head."

The bell over the front door jingled, signaling a new customer. "I'll leave you to it. Let me know if I can help."

Amy found the pregnancy section and picked two for Paige. Then she continued onto the mystery/thriller section. Her father loved to read those. She grabbed a brand-new release from his favorite author and then looked for a cookbook to add to her mother's collection.

Thirty minutes later, she'd gathered almost more books than she could carry. Jamie laughed at the pile beside the cash register. "Did you get everything you needed?"

"That and more, as you can see. You know me in a bookstore. I can't help myself."

"You'll never hear me complain." She rang up the books, placing them in a recycled bag she gave with purchase. After handing back her credit card, Jamie thanked her for the sale.

"Are you kidding? I love your store. Have a Merry Christmas if I don't see you."

"You, too. And I'll see you at the wedding."

"Right. See you then." Paige's wedding was one week from today, and Amy wished she was more excited for it. Or maybe less conflicted. Of course, she was happy for her. She needed to tamp down the growing unease she felt. *What if she lost it at the wedding? Ruined Paige's big day?*

Lost in thought, she slammed into someone on the sidewalk as she left the bookstore.

"Oof. Pardon me," she muttered.

"No damage done."

She looked up into Mac's smiling face. "Hey, what are you doing here?"

He held up a bright red shopping bag. "Probably the same as you. Last-minute gift shopping." He peered down, trying to see in her bag. "Anything for me in there?"

She slid the bag behind her back, grinning. "Mama always said, 'Don't ask questions at Christmas.'"

"Hmmm, I guess I can wait a little longer to see." He leaned down and kissed her on the mouth, stealing her breathe.

"Wow, what was that for?" She put all her energy into not looking around. She didn't want to hurt his feelings, but the last thing she needed was someone seeing them kissing on the street.

"Just an early Christmas gift. Especially since I won't see you for the holiday." He'd already told her he'd volunteered to work, giving coworkers with family the opportunity to be with loved ones.

"What will you do for Christmas dinner?" She hadn't planned anything for them, but it hurt her heart to think of him in the station on Christmas.

"Don't worry about me. Someone always drops off a meal for those of us working. And Kat always brings us an amazing arrangement of her decorated Christmas cookies."

"At least you'll have food."

He tipped her head up with a finger. "Amy, it's okay. This is how I always spend Christmas. Someday, when I have a family, it'll be my turn."

"Right." She couldn't name the funny ache settling in her chest at the thought of him married with children. "Someday. Well, I have to go." She started to turn away, when he caught her by the arm.

"What's wrong?"

She plastered what she hoped was a bright enough smile on her face. If it didn't reach her eyes, she couldn't do anything. "Nothing. I'm fine. I have a lot to do before dinner tonight with my family."

"If you're sure." He leaned down and hugged her. "You know where I am if you need anything. Or you need an ear." Then he wiggled his fiery eyebrows. "Or a bootie call."

She smacked him in the chest with her gloved hand. "I'll keep it in mind, Mr. Mac Gregor." She blamed the frosty air for the heating of her cheeks. "See you around."

Amy walked away while she still could. Before she gave into the temptation to drag him into the nearest warm place for a quickie. Why did thinking of him with a family, with another woman, bother her so much? They were only hanging out, right? Spending time together. She wasn't ready to think of anyone in permanent terms. Was she?

She quickened her pace, boots crunching on the light layer of snow. When she reached her car, she stowed her purchases in the trunk before getting in and cranking the heat. Although winter in the mountains looked like a postcard, she'd take the hot, sunny days of summer. She drove home to wrap her purchases, determined to not think about Mac and their situation. Whatever it might be.

*****

"Where's my lunch?" his partner called as soon as Mac entered the station. He shook his head. For such a tiny person, Trina could out eat most of his guy friends.

"Hold your horses. I'm coming." He entered the kitchen area, determined to not drive himself crazy worrying over things with Amy. But he couldn't help it. Their encounter in town left him with questions. Why had she been eager to rush off? Why had she stiffened when he kissed her? Why didn't her smile quite reach her beautiful eyes?

Trina grabbed the takeout bag from his hands. "What's got your panties in a twist?" She sat down at the table and opened the club sandwich he'd gotten for her.

"What do you mean?" Great, her female radar must be working overtime today.

She stopped, sandwich in midair and glared at him over it. "You're kidding, right? You left here, smiling, whistling a Christmas tune. Then you come back wearing *that* face." She took a large bite and chewed, obviously waiting for an answer.

"There's nothing wrong with my face." Mac turned to the fridge, grabbing waters for both of them. He sat at the opposite end of the table, hoping the small distance would protect him from her endless inquisition.

"Tell me. You know you want to. I'm going to go out on a limb and guess it has something to do with Amy."

No such luck. She was worse than a dog with a bone when she got something on her mind. He sighed and unwrapped his hoagie. "She seemed a little, I don't know, off maybe. No big deal."

"And, yet, it is. What did you do?"

He laughed as he knew she intended. "Why do you always assume it's my fault?"

"Because it usually is. You know I love you, Mac. But you're a guy."

"Gee, what gave it away?"

"The size thirteen work boots. But don't take it personally. It's almost always the guy's fault. Not only you." She grinned before taking another bite.

He put down his lunch. Maybe a female perspective would help. "You know Amy and I have been, uh, hanging out, right?"

"And by that you mean dating."

"Oh, I'm not sure dating is the right word."

"Really? You spend a lot of free time together. Share meals. And sometimes a bed. What would you call it?"

He avoided her gaze and sucked in a breath. *She knew?* "How do you know we're sharing a bed?" He glanced around to make sure they were alone.

She shook her head and muttered something in Spanish which his limited medical training hadn't covered. "Do I look stupid to you?"

"No, of course not."

Trina stood and dragged her lunch to his end of the table before taking the seat next to him. "Honey, I know. Because you're happier these days. And who else would it be?"

"Oh, I uh…no one else knows."

"I'm not going to blab. But out of curiosity, what's the problem? Why don't you want anyone to know?"

He shoved away his lunch. The acid churning in his gut killed his appetite. "I don't have a problem. But I think Amy does."

"What makes you say that?"

"When I kissed her in front of Between the Covers, she stiffened. Like she didn't want me to kiss her on the street."

"Does anyone else know about you guys?"

"Not sure. Probably you and then Paige and Quinn."

"Mac, she's still hurting. This is probably very new to her. Maybe she doesn't want to rush into anything."

"I get it. I do." He ran a hand over his face. "But it's not like I asked her to marry me or anything. I don't know what we're doing, Trina. We have a great time together. Enjoy each other's company. But, well, I can't quite put my finger on it.

Something's not right."

"It's only been a few weeks."

"I know, and it's cool. But we never go out anywhere. Like in public. She comes to my house, or I go to hers. Doesn't it seem strange?"

"You know I love Windsor Falls, but this is a very small town. With a lot of nosy people in it."

He snorted. "Something about a pot calling the kettle black springs to mind." His partner knew everything about everyone. It was kind of scary.

"You leave me out of this. What I was trying to say is everyone knows everything about each other here. Maybe she's not ready for the attention. You know, to go public after losing A.J. Plus, she's a Windsor, so there's added pressure."

"What's that supposed to mean?" He wasn't happy with his tone. And he would pay later for it for sure. But her being a Windsor already rankled with him. He didn't need others pointing it out.

"Hey, slow your roll. All I'm saying is her being a Windsor, in this town, means she's open to even more scrutiny. And that's saying a lot. Maybe she isn't ready to take this public because it's brand new. And she's still getting her feet under her."

"Maybe." He hadn't thought of it like that. And yet, the idea added to the acid in his gut. He was a good guy with his own home and a great career. But he wasn't a Windsor. He didn't have a fancy pedigree or a ton of spare cash. He didn't care about those things, but they might. Her brother certainly would.

His partner covered his hand with her own tiny one. "Slow down. Take a breath. You're only a few weeks into this. Cut her some slack. Give her time to get used to the idea of being with someone else." She stared at him, square in the eye. "And you are fabulous. Amy doesn't care if you're a member of the country club. Give yourself a break while you're at it."

Another thing he loved about her. She always cut right

through the crap. "I will. And thanks. Now let's eat before we get a call."

The words still hung in the air when the overhead tones screeched through the building. Sure enough, it was for them. Motor vehicle accident out on the highway.

Trina looked longingly at her sandwich and took one last, large bite before running for her coat. Mac shoved his lunch back in the bag and left it on the table. Hopefully, he'd have time to eat later.

Chapter Twenty

Amy opened her parent's front door, allowing in a blast of frigid air and Paige and Quinn. She hugged them both. "Come in, come in. Hurry before I freeze."

Paige laughed and dragged Quinn in behind her. "If you had a little more meat on your bones, you wouldn't feel cold." She took off her coat and hung it in the closet. "Where's your mom?"

"In the kitchen of course. Where else would she be?"

"I heard that!" Mrs. Windsor bustled into the foyer, drying her hands on a dish towel. "Paige!" She threw her arms around her friend, as though she hadn't seen her yesterday. "And Quinn, I'm glad you could make it." He got a similar hug.

"Thank you for inviting us, Mrs. Windsor."

"Now, honey, how many times do I have to tell you to call me Susan?"

"Right, Susan. Sorry."

"Did I hear the door?" called Amy's father from his den. Mike Windsor strode into the foyer, shaking Quinn's hand while slapping the younger man on the back. "Who's hungry? Susan hasn't let me in the kitchen to help all day."

"And by help he means eat what I'm making."

"Nothing wrong with it. Everyone needs an official taste tester," her father joked.

"Oh, Mike." Amy watched her petite mother stretch onto her tippy toes to kiss her father's cheek. The scene, witnessed thousands of times throughout her life, never failed to bathe her in happiness. It's what she'd wanted with Andrew. What she'd never have with Andrew. And the sharp pain in her chest, the momentary inability to breathe she'd experienced since his death, failed to materialize. She felt a twinge, maybe a dull ache. But she thought of Mac, and a smile tugged at the corner of her mouth. Mac made her happy.

"I think we lost her," Paige announced from right next to her.

Amy blinked. "What?"

Everyone in the room laughed. Amy felt her cheeks warm. "Sorry, lost in thought, I guess. Mom, what do you need in the kitchen?"

Her mother laughed again. "Nothing from you girls." She turned to the men. "Despite my best attempts, neither is worth a lick in the kitchen. How about y'all set the table for me? Dinner is about done."

"Son, there's our cue to head to the den. Can I get you a drink?"

Quinn nodded. "Anything to avoid helping in the kitchen."

The two men laughed and disappeared into her father's 'man cave' as he referred to it. "Paige, let's get the table." She ventured into the formal dining room. Glancing around the lovely but very stiff room, Amy grimaced. "I'm glad we only eat in here on holidays."

Paige nodded. "I know. It's a beautiful room, but I've never felt comfortable in here."

"Right? Do you remember those awful Sunday brunches in here when Grandmother Windsor was still alive?" She hated to speak ill of the dead, but her father's mother had been the matriarch of the family and took her role very seriously.

"Do I remember? She was forever looking down her nose at me." Paige shuddered. "I never measured up to her standards."

"Me either, but Alex more than made up for our lacking." She stood very straight. "Yes, Grandmother Windsor. Of course, Grandmother Windsor."

"I have never spoken like that in my life," came a not amused masculine voice.

Both women whirled. Her brother stood there in the doorway, arms crossed, scowl on his face. Amy looked at Paige, saw the laughter threatening to leak, and doubled over laughing herself.

"Nice." A disgusted Alex left the dining room.

"Oh. My." She couldn't finish, she laughed so hard.

"I know." Paige dabbed at her eyes. "How Alex ever thought I could marry him. You know I love him like a brother. But, lord, I'd have killed him in the first month."

"Not sure he would have lasted a month."

The two women joked while they finished setting the table. Susan ducked her head into the room. "Are we ready?"

"Yes, ma'am."

"Good. Go call the boys."

Fifteen minutes later, everyone gathered at the table. Her father stood to say grace, and everyone bowed their heads. Amy said a silent prayer of thanksgiving for these people. Each and every one of them. She wasn't sure how she would have gotten through without them. Even Alex, who'd been concerned in his own way. Then she added Mac onto the list.

When the prayer ended, her mother cleared her throat. "Amy, I know you don't want a big fuss made, but I'm happy to have you here with us again for this holiday meal. We all are." There was a general round of agreement with the sentiment. Paige, who cried at the drop of a hat before becoming pregnant, stifled a sob into her fiancée's chest.

"I was thinking how very lucky I am to have you. All of you. And I want you to know I love you all. And thank you for your unwavering support through this, uh, through this most difficult period of my life. Now before we all drown in Paige's tears, can someone pass the stuffing, please?"

"I'm not that bad," Paige protested, while everyone else laughed.

Quinn patted her on the arm. "Yes, you are, honey. But we love you anyway."

Amy watched her friend place a hand across her lower abdomen and wondered if she even knew she was doing it. "Well, this is your fault, so I'm not the only one to blame."

A round of laughter and good-natured ribbing followed, even from Alex, who had thought himself in love with Paige last year. The sound of serving utensils scraping bowls filled the air, competing with different conversations going at once. Amy sat back for a moment, taking it all in. Feeling the cheerful din soothe her battered heart. She'd missed this. She'd stayed away too long. But she'd come back, maybe a bit fragile, maybe a bit scared of the world, but she'd come back. She thought of Mac, wondering if he was at the station eating dinner or maybe out on a call, saving someone's Christmas. And she sent a thought into the universe to keep him safe and warm.

*****

Across town, Mac wiped down the now empty stretcher, readying it for their next call. They never knew when someone would need them. Their elderly patient had eaten a bit too much rich holiday food and had a terrible case of indigestion. Much better than the heart attack his family thought he suffered. He accepted their thanks and shrugged off an apology. Always better to be safe than sorry.

Once the rig was straightened, he ducked back into the warm ER. Tonight's record-breaking temperatures were hard to take. As long as they didn't have a call, he might as well snag a snack. ERs were infamous for their abundance of holiday food.

Turning a corner, he almost knocked over Elizabeth, one of his friends and favorite ER doctors. He reached, grabbing her arms to prevent her from falling.

"Sorry, Mac, and thank you for saving me." She rubbed her rounded belly. "This little one is taking away my coordination. Not that I had much to begin with." She hugged the taller man, reaching up to kiss his cheek.

"You look beautiful, like last time. Any idea who you might be carrying in there yet?"

"It's way too early to tell. Don't tell Sam, but I'm hoping for a girl."

"One of each. That would be awesome. How do you think Gabriel will feel about being a big brother?"

"Who knows? They will be very close in age, but then I'm not getting any younger. Neither is Sam."

"Ah, he'll be fine. They'll be each other's best friends." He'd always wanted a sibling, so his view might be a bit one-sided.

"And worst enemies. I remember the Fitzgerald clan when we were all growing up. Those kids could fight to the death. And not only the boys. But you'd better not be someone outside the family making trouble with any of them. Then you'd have the whole bunch on your head."

"It sounds wonderful. I always wanted a sibling or two."

"When are you going to settle down and have a family of your own?"

"First, I have to find the right woman. And since Sam already snatched you away from me." He shrugged his massive shoulders. "Guess I'll have to try internet dating."

Elizabeth shuddered. "Don't do it. I've heard horror stories from some of the younger nurses here. I couldn't be single again." She cocked her head, looking up into his eyes. "What about Amy Windsor? I thought you two were 'talking' as the young folks put it."

Mac shuffled his feet, not sure how to answer. "I wish I knew." The radio on his belt squawked, saving him from a longer answer. He snagged a handful of cookies from the counter and yelled for Trina. "Gotta go. Have a great Christmas if I don't see you again, Elizabeth."

"You, too, Mac. I'm heading home now. I won't be here if

you bring another one in." She wagged a finger at him. "And don't think I'm going to settle for a half-baked answer." She laughed as she walked away.

He headed out into the frigid air, thinking about the question. Elizabeth wasn't the first to ask him about Amy in the past week. And knowing how the rumor mill in Windsor Falls worked, she wouldn't be the last. But it didn't change the fact he didn't have an answer.

Turning on the truck, he jacked the heat and waited for it to take the bite out of the air. Trina jumped into the front, and he took off.

"What were you and the doctor talking about? You looked as thick as thieves, as my dead grandmother would say."

"This and that. Mostly about her pregnancy."

"And she didn't happen to ask you about Amy?"

He stared straight ahead, but the tone of his partner's voice told him exactly the look he would have found on her face. Humor and disbelief. He sighed. "Are all women psychic?"

"I'll take it as a yes," she answered with a smug tone. "What did you tell her?"

"I was saved by the bell. Literally."

"Mac."

He sighed. "I don't know what she and I are doing. And I don't want to scare her away by asking too many questions or pressuring her. For now, we're hanging out."

"A little 'friends with benefits.'"

"Hey, don't say that. I really hate the expression."

"Interesting."

He waited for something else, but she stopped talking. "God knows I'll regret this, but what do you mean?"

"It's interesting you don't like the term in connection with Amy, when I've heard you use it before. Interesting you're not pushing her for answers to avoid pushing her away. Interesting you get really tense when I mention her name. That's all."

He pulled the truck into the driveway of the address dispatch had given them. He turned to her for a brief moment. "You're right on each. I don't know what I'm doing. I care about her. A lot. And it's early days. I'm taking it a day at a time. Okay?"

He expected banter but met a solemn face. "I like Amy. I always have. But if she hurts you, she's dead meat." She left the truck before he could begin to answer. Didn't matter. There wasn't anything he could say.

Chapter Twenty-One

The next afternoon, Amy pulled open the side door to the fire station. She'd sat in her car first. For almost an hour. The last time she'd been here was the day they buried Andrew. It took every bit of courage she possessed, and more than she knew she had, just to open the door. Now, feeling a little lost and silly, she looked around the cavernous bays. Gleaming trucks sat empty, pointed at the doors as if awaiting the next call.

"Hello?" she called out, her voice echoing through the space.

"Hey," came a female voice. A petite, Hispanic woman came around a corner. Amy searched her memory for the woman's name. This had to be Mac's partner.

She walked toward her. "Trina, right?"

"Yes." The other woman closed the gap. "Nice to see you again, Amy."

Before she could reply, the other woman wrapped her in a hug. "Oh." She stood there, not sure how to respond.

Trina released her, taking a step back and laughed. "You'll get used to me. I hug everyone. Are you looking for Mac?"

She was, of course, but standing here with his partner, in his place of work, she felt a bit stupid. She shifted the wrapped box from one hand to the other. "Oh, yes, of course, but if he's busy... I, uh, wanted to give him this."

"He took the truck to fill it with gas. He'll be right back. Why don't you come inside?"

"Oh, I don't know." But Trina already turned and walked away, clearly expecting her to follow. So, she did. The other woman entered the kitchen and pulled out a chair for Amy.

"Would you like something to drink?"

"Water if you have it. Thank you." She undid her coat, unwrapping her scarf as well. The temperature inside must have been close to seventy.

Trina laughed and pulled a bottle from the fridge, handing it to her. "I can't stand the cold. I always crank the heat when I'm working. Mac hates it. Which is as good a reason as any to do it."

"I like you already," Amy said.

"What are your intentions with my partner?"

The question caught her off guard and sent her scrambling to answer. Variations of a response bounced through her mind when Trina burst into laughter.

"Geez, your face, Amy!" She doubled over for a moment before straightening and sliding into a chair at the table. "I was kidding. Well, sort of. Mac is like another big brother. Mind you, I have five."

"Five older brothers? Wow. I only have one, and there are days I want to strangle him."

"And now I like you, too. Believe me, there are days. And Mac is no better. Always giving me crap about something. But he does it out of love, you know?"

The expression in her dark eyes left no room for doubt. The warning was there, even if subtle. "I do know. It's nice he has someone watching out for him."

"Should I ask what you two are discussing?" came his baritone from the doorway.

A herd of butterflies took flight in her belly. She took a sip of water, more for something to do with her hands then out of thirst.

"I was telling your *friend* here how much you remind me of one of my brothers. And how family always sticks together."

"Trina." His warning tone brought a smile to Amy's face. She was grateful he had someone watching his back.

"Well, I have to get back to my episode of *Supernatural*. Jensen Ackles. Yummy!" She ducked out of the room before he could say anything else.

"I'm sorry for whatever she might have said to you. Trina is, well, she's right. She is family. She gets a bit overprotective sometimes."

The thought of the tiny woman defending the big, strapping paramedic brought a smile to her lips. "I get it. Family is important. I'm glad you have her."

"We're all a family here, the fire guys and us. A.J. was a part of our family. I hope you know this."

"I do, and it makes me happy knowing how loved he was." She looked at the floor for a moment, unsure what else to say.

"Is this for me?"

"What?" Amy brought her gaze up, landing on the present. "Oh, yes, of course. Sorry, I forgot it for a moment."

"But I don't have your present with me. I didn't think I'd see you today."

She stood, coming around the table to stand next to him. "Its's okay. I spent the night with my parents and was on my way home. Thought I'd take a chance. Go ahead, open it."

"Now? But you don't have yours."

"No worries. You can give it to me another time. Open it. Go ahead."

He picked up the box, and the fluttering in her belly increased. She clasped her hands together, hoping he'd like it. "It's really nothing. Just a little something I thought you'd like."

His hands stilled on the wrapping paper. "You thought of me. It's all that matters."

She smiled and held her breath while he finished opening

the paper.

"It's a box," he exclaimed with a smile.

"What gave it away?"

"I wonder what's inside." He opened the box and pulled out the mug she'd bought him. It didn't seem like such a great gift now, in front of him. Kind of impersonal.

"I love it." He set the mug on the table and wrapped her in his arms. His scent, a touch of cold air mixed with clean, strong male, tickled her nose. She hugged him in return.

"I noticed you have quite a few at your place."

"But not a single one with the Clan Mac Gregor family crest on it."

She glanced at the red and blue tartan pattern surrounding the crest, pleased with her choice again. "It's a strong name, Mac Gregor. Rich in history. I thought you might enjoy this."

"Where did you find it? I've never seen one around here."

"Oh, I Googled it and found a place."

"Whatever did we do before Google? Seriously, Amy, I love it. Thank you. And please ignore whatever Trina might have said to you."

"I heard," echoed in from the other room.

"You were meant to," he answered with a smile on his face, his affection for her written in his expression.

"It's not a big deal. I, uh, should probably go. I didn't mean to bother you at work."

He took a few steps, until he trapped her against the table. Her pulse throbbed in her throat. "You're never bothering me, Amy. And I love that you thought about me. Really." He held up the mug. "I'll think of you every time I drink coffee."

Whatever else he might have said was interrupted by the loud overhead bells. Mac laughed. "There's my cue." He leaned in, giving her a brief but fierce kiss. "I'll call you when I get a moment."

She stood there, bones melting, and nodded. Watched him run to the truck. Amy waited for them to leave before going herself. She rode home with a smile on her face.

*****

Thick, grey clouds gathered, blotting out the weak sun from earlier. Snow started to fall. "Things might get messy before we get off tonight," he said to his partner.

A snort greeted him. "Really? You're going to talk about the weather? The woman you've been mooning over for weeks stops by unannounced with a Christmas gift, and you want to talk about the weather." She shook her head.

"Do I have a choice?" He knew he didn't but liked to mess with her.

"Of course not. Tell me everything. What did she get you?"

"Amy bought me a coffee mug with my family crest on it. Not sure where she found one, but I like it. Means she thought about me." He didn't try to stop the grin spreading across his face. "I hadn't expected any gift at all. Go ahead. Make fun of it. Or me. I'm in too good of a mood."

"I think it's nice. And you're right, she put some thought into it. Knows coffee runs in your veins apparently. And personalized it. Nice touch. What are you going to get her?"

"I, uh, already did. You know, just in case." He kept their truck on the road despite the force with which she hit his arm. "What was that for?"

"Nice going, Mac. Really. I didn't think you had it in you. What did you get her? You didn't mess it up, did you?"

"Meaning?"

"Well, you, like most men, are kind of clueless when it comes to gift giving. On second thought, tell me what you got her before I judge you."

"Just because Manny bought you something for the house one year, doesn't mean we're all stupid. Or suicidal."

"Hangers! The man bought me hangers." She rambled off in rapid fire Spanish. Mac knew better than to interrupt. After a moment, she grinned. "Sorry. The memory of it makes my blood boil."

"In his defense, they were really nice, padded hangers.

You know, the kind that doesn't stretch your clothing. At least it's what he told me."

"They were still hangers. Back to you."

"If you must know, I bought her earrings. They're silver and have a stone that matches her eyes."

A low whistle filled the cab of the truck. "Nicely done, my friend. I'm impressed."

"Would you like me to give your husband some pointers?" he joked.

"Nah. He's gotten better. Something about sleeping on the couch showed him the light. But thanks."

"That's what partners are for." He shifted in the seat. "Do they sound okay for her? The earrings?"

"They sound terrific. Jewelry is always a good choice. And earrings aren't over the top personal at this point in the relationship. Unless they're butt ugly, you should be okay."

"Why would I buy her something 'butt ugly'?"

"Maybe I'd better see them first. Before you give them to her."

He shook his head as he pulled to the edge of the accident scene. "I'll take my chances." Surveying the scene before he left the safety of their vehicle, all small talk ended. "Let's go."

The light snow had created a thin, icy layer on the roads. There'd be more of these calls before his shift ended. A small car had skidded across the street, ending in a crash into a parked vehicle. On this type of small, side street, with low speed limits, damage was generally light. But you never knew.

They both left the truck. One police car sat off to the side, the officer at the driver's window. He approached him. "Hey, Rob, what do we have?"

The newest member of the Windsor Falls force turned to greet him. Mac wasn't sure he was old enough to shave, let alone carry a gun. "Hey, Mac. Uh, I'm not sure. There weren't any skid marks. Can't get her to answer me."

Mac approached the car. "Trina, this may be something more than an MVA." He knocked on the window. "Ma'am, can you hear me?" The driver lay upright in her seat, face turned away from them. She didn't answer. "We're going to need to gain access. Try all the doors."

None budged. One disadvantage of newer models with automated locks. "Rob, can you grab your Slim Jim? We need to get into this car. Sooner rather than later."

The younger man nodded and picked his way over the ice back to his patrol car. Mac glanced across the roof to Trina. "Can you see any movement from her?"

"Nah. But she's definitely breathing. Looks shallow though."

"Come on, Rob, hurry," he called to the officer. Knocking again, Mac yelled louder this time. "Ma'am, open your eyes." Nothing.

Rob came back, and Mac, already feeling the ticking of the clock, grabbed the tool from his hand. "Let me." He maneuvered the thin piece of metal down along the window frame, moving it back and forth until he heard the lock pop. He removed the tool, tossing it to the ground before yanking open the door. Reaching across their patient, he slid the control to park and turned off the car. The first thing he noticed was the fruity smell to her breath. He hit the unlock button, allowing Trina to enter from the passenger side.

"Smell something funny?"

"Yep. Someone hasn't eaten lately."

Mac nodded. The overly sweet smell to her breath led them both to guess the driver had lost consciousness to a drop in her blood sugar. Her altered mental status let them know it had dropped dangerously low. "Grab a blood sugar right away. And have dextrose ready."

While his partner tested one finger for a reading, he shined his penlight in their patient's face. "Hey, are you with me? Open your eyes." The woman moaned but didn't follow his commands.

"Thirty, Mac. I'm giving the glucagon before I start an IV."

"Great." Knowing Trina had the emergency treatment

covered, Mac started a head to toe assessment. Their patient had sweaty skin and a pale tone that screamed low blood sugar. He didn't see any further complications. She was breathing on her own, at least for now. As gently as he could, he removed one arm from her coat and sweater. After starting an IV, he added a bag of fluids with glucose to further raise her low level.

A few moments later, the older woman began to arouse. "What's going on?" Although her speech remained a bit slurred, he was happy she responded at all.

"Welcome back, ma'am. I'm Mac, and this is Trina. We're with EMS. You've had a small accident."

"I don't remember." Her eyes drifted closed for a moment before popping back open. "Where am I?"

"Don't worry, we've got you," Mac said in his calmest tone. Sometimes the best thing they could do for a patient was offer support in a scary time. "Your blood sugar plummeted, but we're working on it. Are you feeling any better?"

The woman attempted a small smile at him. "I am. Oh, I'm so foolish. I'm getting over a stomach bug, and I haven't been able to eat much."

"But you continued your regular insulin, didn't you?" The scenario was one he'd seen many times. People forgot to adjust their insulin for decreased intake. "Be thankful the accident wasn't worse. But we do need to take you to the hospital."

"Oh, please don't fuss over me."

Mac explained about the accident and the need to be checked out more thoroughly. After a few more moments of fussing on her part, they loaded her up and drove to the ER. Trina rode in back with their patient, giving him plenty of time to ponder when to give Amy her present. *Why hadn't he brought it with him to the station?* No use worrying. Plus, he'd never imagined her stopping by. It was a good thing, he hoped. Amy coming to see him at work, out in the open and all, had to mean things were looking up. And the perfect time to give her the Christmas gift came to him.

Chapter Twenty-Two

Only a few moments of Christmas remained when Amy's phone buzzed with a text. Surprised at the late hour, she glanced down at it, sitting on her nightstand.

"Can I come in?" A Santa emoji followed, making her laugh.

Her heart rate quickened as she bounded out of bed, stopping long enough only to smooth back her hair. She rushed to the door and then out to the main one, pulling it open. Mac and a burst of freezing air swept in. He picked her up off her feet, swinging her around in his arms and giving his best 'Ho, ho, ho'.

Amy laughed as he set her back down. "Come in, it's freezing out there." She led the way inside, shutting and locking the door after her. "You're up late."

"So are you, and I'm glad." He stepped in, his lips the only point of contact as he kissed her.

She didn't feel the least bit chilled anymore. Amy leaned into the kiss, needing more. She wrapped her arms around him until there wasn't any space left between them. And the kiss exploded. Shock waves of sensation raced through her body, curling her bare toes. She finally broke the kiss only when a need for oxygen trumped all else.

"Wow." Mac reached into the pocket of his work coat and pulled out a small, wrapped box. "Sorry I'm late. I worked a double and then raced home to grab this. Sorry, too, for not having it with me earlier." He brushed a swath of hair from her face, his hand chilled against her skin.

"You didn't have to." She plucked the rectangular box from his hand, plopping down on the couch. "But I'm glad you did. I love gifts."

Mac laughed at her childlike exuberance as she ripped into the wrapping paper. He took off his coat and sat next to her, turning toward her to watch her expression.

She took the lid off the box and pushed tissue paper aside. "Oh, Mac, they're beautiful!" She took out the earrings and slid them into the holes in her ears, turning to face him again. She lifted the hair from her neck. "What do you think?"

"I think I chose well," he joked.

She hit him with a couch pillow. "True but not the answer I was looking for."

He leaned in and looked straight into her eyes. "They look beautiful on you." He sealed it with another kiss, leaving her breathless.

"That's better. I really do love them. You shouldn't have. This makes my gift seem, I don't know, lacking somehow."

He covered her hands with his. "Not at all. I love that you took the time to think of me and get me something personalized. I do."

"Well, then you're going to love the next part of your gift." She stood next to the couch and reached down for his hand. No words were needed. He followed her into her bedroom.

Once inside, she closed the door. "Keep in mind, if I knew you were coming over, I'd have dressed more carefully." She took off her oldest, most comfortable robe, laying it across the back of a chair.

He glanced down at the old T-shirt which barely grazed the top of her knees. "What you're wearing takes my breath away. I'm not sure I would have handled anything else." He walked toward her, removing his work belt as he went. When he had backed her against the side of the bed, he pushed her shoulders enough to topple her onto the bed. "Better."

Amy lay on the bed, breath quickening. She glanced up at him as he began to remove his clothing. "Want some help?"

"No thanks. I'll get to you next." He continued his slow, impromptu striptease until only his underwear remained. Then he dropped to his knees on the floor in front of her. One large hand pushed each knee aside.

She raised up on her elbows in order to see him. Moisture pooled in her core. Heat crept from her belly outward. She licked her lips. "Mac?"

He didn't respond, only pulled her until her butt reached the end of the bed. Then he pulled the edge of her shirt upward, exposing her cotton underwear. "Red. How Christmassy. I like it. But it has to go." Using both hands, he stripped the brief material down and off her body. "Even better."

He'd barely touched her, and she already felt like exploding. Amy threw her head back. "Please, touch me."

"Oh, I will."

She felt his hot breath on her thighs and opened them further without thought. He kissed the inside of each one, and she gripped the comforter on either side of her. "More," she muttered between clenched jaws.

A masculine chuckle followed by the swipe of his tongue answered her plea. Her hips jacked off the bed in response. "Oh. Yes, Mac, right there."

He swirled his tongue faster, deeper inside her, circling the sensitive bud hiding there. Just one touch, and her muscles shook. She spread her legs apart further, giving him more access. He inserted a finger deep inside her, playing with the very core of her.

"I need you now. All of you. Inside me."

He shook his head. "Next time," he growled before sliding his tongue back inside and feasting on her.

It was more than she could bear. She clenched her eyes

shut against the fireworks exploding within in her. Her legs quivered. She panted through her release. She felt rather than saw him move. Before she could open her eyes, he swept her in his arms and pulled back the comforter. He laid her in the middle of the bed and grabbed something from his pants on the floor.

She opened her eyes to see him ripping open a condom wrapper. She held out one hand.

Mac smiled and dropped it in her hand then laid down next to her. "I want to feel you all around me," he whispered into her ear.

Her hands shook as she unwrapped the condom. She slid it down the length of him, taking her time, playing with him along the way. His hissed in breath was all the encouragement she needed. "No one wants it more than I do," she answered.

He leaned over her, taking one breast in his mouth, teasing and sucking the tight bud. She felt it right to her very core, as though a wire stretched taught between the two places. She reached between them, taking ahold of him, and caressed the length of him. He released her breast, blowing cool air on the peak.

"Now, please," she whispered to him, even as she continued to stroke his length.

He didn't have to be told again. Mac freed himself from her loose grip and poised over her. He stared into her eyes as he lowered himself closer. She felt the tip of him nudge her curls, asking for entry. She raised her hips, meeting him, inviting him inside her.

Whatever control he might have had shattered with her act. Mac slid into her in one stroke until he buried the length of himself in her heat. She clenched him from inside, enjoying the noises coming from him. She watched the muscles of his shoulders tighten as he reared back and plunged in once again. The friction where they met set her in motion, climbing toward another release. She moaned his name, drawing the one syllable out.

"Say it again," he commanded.

She stared at him. "Mac, I need you now."

He quickened the tempo, setting a lightning fast pace, moving in and out of her. Each plunge brought her closer and closer to the edge of the cliff. She was right there, so close, when he rubbed her with his thumb. The one, small act sent her hurtling over the edge. Tiny zaps of electricity burned her throughout her body, raced along her nerve endings. She tried to close her eyes on the waves of feeling.

"Look at me," he whispered to her.

She opened her eyes, finding his face right above hers. He captured her lips, stroking her tongue with his, as he stroked her down below. She felt his muscles tightening. And a warm rush of him entered her.

Mac collapsed half on top of her, pulling her into his chest. "My kind of Christmas gift," he joked into her hair.

She glanced at the small, antique clock on her bedside table. "It's not even Christmas anymore." She kissed his face, enjoying the salty taste to his skin. Reveling in the fact she made it happen.

"Then merry day after Christmas to you. Save my spot." He got up and disappeared into the bathroom.

Amy rolled over, clenching her inner muscles against the aftershocks rolling through her body. She'd missed the contact, the highs of great sex. She lay in the dark waiting for him to return. She enjoyed this part as much. Lying in bed with him afterwards, falling asleep in his arms. She'd missed the human contact more than anything. Something chilled slid through her chest. It was too soon to depend on him. They'd only known each other a few weeks, even less for this level of involvement. *Was she really willing to risk it again?*

As if conjuring him, Mac slid under the covers, gathering her against his chest. He brushed aside some hair. "I love these earrings even more when they're all you're wearing." He sealed it with a kiss in the oh so sensitive spot behind one ear.

She shivered in response. "I bet you do." A yawn escaped her. "Sorry, it's been a long day. And I have a lot to do with

Paige tomorrow. With Christmas over, she's really freaking out." She felt him stiffen behind her and closed her eyes on the hurt.

"Do you want me to leave?"

NO! she screamed in her mind but nodded. "I need some sleep."

"No worries." He kissed her cheek before sliding back out of bed.

She heard him dress in the dark behind her but refused to turn. If she looked at him, she'd beg him to stay. "I'm sure you have plenty to do with Quinn."

"I guess. Although you ladies always have a bigger to-do list when it comes to weddings."

"True," she murmured, settling further into her pillow. She needed him to go before she lost all control.

He rounded the bed, leaning down to kiss her forehead. "I'll call you tomorrow. Or later today I guess."

"Okay, great." She closed her eyes to avoid seeing him walk away. Asking him to leave didn't make it any easier to watch him go. She held her breath until she heard the soft snick of her front door closing. She let it out, shuddering at the thought of sending him away. She missed him already and buried her nose in the sheets.

*****

Mac cursed under his breath as the freezing temps stole his breath. He ran to his truck and started it, praying the heater would kick in. But the temperature had dropped in the time he'd been inside, and his less than ten-minute ride home would be spent freezing.

Just another thing to add to his bad mood. He pulled out onto the street and headed home, wishing he still lay in a nice, warm bed, cuddled up to Amy. What had gone wrong? She seemed more than happy to see him, if their sex was any indication. Yet, here he was heading home in the middle of the night. Everything felt like one step forward, one to the side with her lately. Was she regretting sleeping with him? Or maybe coming to his work today? Was he somehow putting too much pressure on her?

He ground his molars and turned onto his street. He was more than on his way to falling in love with her. He was happy he hadn't fucked up and blurted it out to her. Well, not happy exactly. But if the thought of spending the night with him had her kicking him out, what would revealing his feelings for her cause? Besides, these were early days. They had nothing but time. She'd come around, right? He wanted to believe it, but the icy fingers wrapping around his heart challenged the dropping temperature outside.

He pulled into his driveway, about to make a beeline for the warmth of inside, when the slightest noise caught his attention. He stopped and listened again, not sure he'd heard anything. Nothing. He took another few steps, only to hear the strange sound once more. Closer this time, it seemed to be coming from the bushes near his front porch. Mac hit the flashlight app on his phone and shined it in the area. Two big, frightened eyes glowed back at him.

Mac hunched down next to the bush and extended his fingers toward the frightened critter. Without warning, the tiny puppy launched itself at him, landing in a heap at his boots. With a light yip, the dirt-covered animal cocked its head and looked up at Mac as if to say 'hello.'

Without thinking, he scooped up the shivering puppy and carried it inside. Heading straight to the laundry off the kitchen, he placed the tiny puppy in the sink and grabbed some old towels he used for workouts. Since the little guy, or maybe girl, already shivered to beat the band, he rubbed it with a towel to brush off the dirt he could. No use adding water to the mix right now.

Gently rubbing away layers of dirt and grime, not to mention a few twigs, he discovered he was indeed a boy. And probably part German Shepherd from the markings. He wrapped the puppy in a clean towel and held it up to his face. A small, pink tongue darted out to lick his chin.

"Oh, no you don't. I'm not falling for your cute tricks. I'm happy to keep you here tonight, give you something to eat. But in the morning, you have to go. I'm not sure where, but I don't have time for a dog right now."

Apparently unfazed by Mac's warning, his new friend yipped one more time before burrowing into his chest and falling asleep with a sigh.

"Great. Now what do I do?" It had been a very long time since he owned a dog. He could ask Sam, but the other man might not appreciate being awoken at this late hour. He grabbed a box from the pantry and placed a few clean towels in it then carried the nest into his master bathroom.

He placed the puppy in the box, leaving a small light burning for him before walking into his bedroom. Exhaustion from the double shift caught up with him. Mac stripped to his underwear, shivering before diving into his bed. Nothing like flannel sheets on a cold, winter night he thought before feeling sleep slide over him.

And then a series of yips and yaps sounded from the bathroom. He didn't know much about puppies, but weren't you supposed to let them cry it out? It seemed like a good idea until five minutes later when the puppy added howls to his repertoire.

"All right, all right," he called to his new friend. Reluctantly, he left his nice, warm bed and entered the bathroom. He grabbed the box, puppy and all, and carried it back into his bedroom. Placing the box next to him on the floor, he got back into bed once again. Stretching out on his belly, he dangled one arm over the edge of the bed, fingers resting on the box.

"Now, listen. This is all I'm going to offer. Take it or leave it."

The nameless puppy, Mac knew better than to name it, stared at him for a moment before licking his fingers. Then he curled up in a ball in the old towels. He fell asleep within seconds.

"Must be tiring, being a puppy. Making all this racquet,"

Mac grunted at him. He pulled the comforter up around his neck. "Good-night," he whispered to the sleeping puppy. This sure wasn't the way he'd planned on ending his night.

Chapter Twenty-Three

The rest of the week passed in a blur for Amy. She wasn't kidding when she said Paige had a lot to do before the wedding. Because they'd planned it in less than a month, all the traditional vendors had been booked. It was only by some miracle the Mountain Lodge had a small room available for both the wedding and reception. Other than food, drinks, and cake, everything else fell to them. And neither one of them was at all crafty. Luckily, they had many friends who were.

And this was the great thing about living in a small town. People had come from everywhere to lend a hand. Amy's mom, Susan, belonged to a quilting group. So here they sat, in her mother's house, making ribbons and other decorations for the wedding. Which was tomorrow night.

Paige had made it through her final fitting, but only barely. She'd gained a few pounds this month while eating for two. Her dress fit, but it was a bit snugger than her friend cared for. Which had resulted in a flood of tears. Her mother, never one to cry alone, joined in. But in the end, the dress fit. Paige looked beautiful, and all was well. One disaster handled. She was sure there would be more.

"Amy, dear, your ribbon looks a bit, uh, lopsided." Jane, a friend of her mother's from the group, took the offending heap of ribbon from her hands. "Let me fix it."

"Please do. Mom will tell you I'm not any good at these things."

"I'm happy to tell you my darling daughter never wanted to sit still long enough to learn."

She stuck her tongue out at her mother but laughed. It was the honest truth. She'd never learned to cook or sew like her mother could. She and Paige had always preferred to be outside doing something, anything, else.

"In Amy's defense," Paige began. "I'm hopeless as well." She held up a glob of grey, satin ribbon.

Her mother crossed the room, taking the ribbon out of Paige's hands. "Why don't you girls go make yourselves a snack. We've got this."

"Great. Can I get you ladies anything?" She wasn't one to look a gift horse in the mouth., and made her escape to the kitchen, all but dragging Paige behind her. "Whew. That was close."

Paige slumped onto a kitchen chair. "Thank you. I was about to fall asleep in a pile of ribbon." She stretched and yawned, covering her mouth as she did. "Late afternoon is not my best time these days."

"Good thing we took care of the rehearsal this morning then." Standing there, at the pretend altar, so close to him, had turned her knees to mush. She hadn't spoken to Mac since he left her home, at her request, on Christmas night. Her own fault. But it didn't make the bitter pill any easier to swallow.

"Awwww," Paige crooned while looking at something on her phone. "Looks like Finn got himself a new playmate."

"What are you talking about?"

Paige turned the phone toward her, showing a picture of a cute black and tan puppy. "Cute. Who's puppy?"

"This is Gus. Because apparently, he looks like a Gus, at least according to Mac."

"What does Mac have to do with naming Gus? And again, who is Gus? As in, to whom does he belong?"

"He's Mac's new dog. How do you not know?"

"Mac doesn't have a dog." She spoke slowly, trying to solve the riddle in her own mind.

"He didn't, and now he does. And again, how do you not know?"

She didn't answer Paige right away, not sure what to say. The past few days had flown by with wedding stuff to organize. The few times her friend had asked about Mac, she answered in vague nothings. She certainly hadn't mentioned kicking the man out of bed in the dead of night.

"What aren't you telling me? I thought things seemed, uh, strange between you guys this morning. Spill."

Amy grabbed juice from the fridge, pouring two glasses for them before sitting down at the table. Stalling, if truth be told. "I, uh, haven't seen much of him this week. He certainly didn't mention getting a puppy." The fact that he had a new dog and didn't tell her sent a shaft of pain through her chest. But then again, also her fault.

"Try telling me the truth. The whole truth. Did you guys have another fight? Honestly, I can't imagine why y'all can't get along."

If she only knew. "It was nothing really." She hoped not, crossing her fingers under the table.

"If it was nothing, then why aren't you talking? And why didn't you tell me about it?"

And then she did. In one long, run-on sentence she spilled everything. From their morning runs to falling into bed with him to kicking him out of bed in the freezing night. She whispered most of it, due to the older ladies in the next room. When she finished the whole sordid tale, Amy collapsed back against her chair and sipped some juice.

"Why didn't you tell me?" The always present tears slid down Paige's face. For a moment, Amy only felt jealousy at the ability to release emotion. *Why couldn't she cry?*

"I wanted to. I did. In fact, I started to tell you so many times. But I didn't want you to overreact."

"I wouldn't," she sobbed into a paper towel.

"Really," replied Amy in the driest tone possible.

Paige blew her nose and gave a watery smile. "Okay, I have been a bit unhinged with all these hormones swimming around inside of me. I give you that."

"The truth is I didn't know what to say. I'm not even sure what I'm feeling. How do I explain it to you?"

"Do you love him?"

"What? No! Of course not." The idea of her falling in love again, opening herself up to tremendous pain again. Losing someone again. She shook her head several times.

"But you care about him, right? I've known you, Amy, your whole life. You wouldn't have slept with him if you didn't care about him."

"You're right, and I do care about him." The very thought of him, leaving her in the dark because she asked him to, sent a wave of acid through her gut.

"Then why are you afraid? He's not Andrew. He isn't going to die on you."

"How do you know?" She clenched her eyes shut, remembering the last time she saw him. Kissing him that morning on his way out the door. Not knowing she'd never see him again. "Andrew promised me he wouldn't die on me. And he did." The last few words came out a raw whisper. She clutched her throat.

"Oh, honey." A fresh sheen of tears showed in Paige's eyes. "No one can make such a promise. And Andrew shouldn't have. But Mac doesn't run into burning buildings."

"No, he doesn't. It doesn't mean he can't get killed in the line of duty. Or hit by a car crossing the street."

"Same is true for you. And yet he seems to really care about you."

"I know. I have to think about this." She smiled at her very best friend in the whole world. "But first, let's get you married tomorrow. Afterward, there will be plenty of time to figure out my life."

*****

"The Wedding March" played as Paige walked toward them, down the aisle. Mac knew he should be focused on the bride, but the gorgeous maid of honor across the small space held his attention. Although he'd seen her dress before, seeing her today, with her blonde hair piled on her head and delicate silver heels on her feet, he'd struggled for air when he first caught sight of her.

Then she smiled at him, and the knot in his chest loosened a bit. She'd reached the minister and turned to her side. But right before, and only for a moment, she smiled at him. Not at Quinn or anyone else. And the knot began to unfurl. She hadn't tossed him aside. They would talk later, dance a little, maybe have a few drinks. And he would make her see there was nothing to fear. Feeling better about everything, he turned to watch his best friend's fiancée walk toward him.

Paige's smile lit the room. He'd known, from the first time he saw the two together, something was there; something special between them. And here they were, all ready to watch the two exchange vows. He sighed when Paige joined Quinn before the minister. They made sense together. The way he hoped he and Amy might. Someday.

The short ceremony ended with a blistering kiss and more than a few wolf whistles from the audience. You couldn't predict what a first responder might do. There were a few moments of mad cheering with hugs and kisses before everyone moved to the tables set around the perimeter of the room.

Mac immediately sought out Amy, finding her standing to the side, holding the bride's flowers. Despite not being the bride, she was the most beautiful woman in the room. He wouldn't mention it to Quinn. He started toward her, hoping to touch her for the first time in a week.

"Hey there," he murmured to her, kissing her cheek. "Have you ever seen two people look happier?"

"No, I haven't. And they both deserve it and much more."

"Well, the 'much more' is already in the works."

"True." She sighed and turned to him. "I'm sorry for the other night. I don't know what came over me. I, uh, well, I wish I could take it all back."

"I'd rather you tell me what's going on, Amy. Talk to me. Help me to understand. Just don't shut me out. Please."

She started to respond, but her Great Aunt Matilda interrupted. "Oh my, didn't Paige look a dream?" She glanced at Mac. "And is this your young man? Will the two of you be next, dear?"

Before she could answer, her parents came and collected Great Aunt Matilda, who liked to have one too many at these occasions. She smiled her thanks to them, but her aunt's words reverberated in her ears.

Paige appeared at her side. "Now for the fun part," she joked. "Mac, doesn't Amy look stunning tonight? Good thing she's my best friend, or I might have to hate her for showing up the bride."

Mac stepped into her, kissing her cheek. "You have nothing to worry about. You look stunning."

A faint blush crept across her cheeks. "I'll take the compliment and hold onto it when I'm so pregnant, I can't see my own feet." She hugged him. "Now, let me find my new husband and get these pictures out of the way." She took her bouquet from Amy's suddenly cold hands and turned away.

"Amy, is something wrong?"

"I need some air."

But Jack blocked her path. She glanced at the tall, handsome man who had worked with Andrew. "Where are you off to in such a rush? I wanted to say hello. Haven't had a chance to talk to you since, well, since that day." He glanced at Mac, probably feeling the weight of his stare. "Don't worry, man, I'm not after your girl."

Mac watched Amy stiffen. But before he could say anything, she took off after the bride. "Nice going," he all but growled at Jack.

The other man looked at him with a blank expression on his face. "What? I know she's here with you. Don't worry. I won't hit on her."

Mac drew up to his full height, glowering at the shorter man. "Least of my concerns." He went off in search of her.

But even when he found her, she remained distant throughout the evening. Despite being seated next to her at dinner, he didn't have a chance to talk to her about anything other than the wedding. Her taut face, with its frozen smile, worried him. But they had time. Plenty of time. At least he hoped.

*****

Amy glanced at her phone for what seemed like the thousandth time and wondered, once again, if she could leave yet. She instantly regretted the thought. She loved Paige with every fiber of her being and wanted only the best for her, but she had to leave. The constant happiness and good cheer echoed in her empty chest. She'd be fine once the wedding was over. She'd keep telling herself until the words rang true.

"I'm beginning to think you're avoiding me," drawled a deep, masculine tone from behind her. She didn't have to turn to know the owner. Chills danced up and down her spine.

"I am the maid of honor. Paige needs me for things." She glanced out to the dance floor, where the new husband and wife danced together without a thought of anyone else in the world, let alone the crowd gathered.

"Well, I think Quinn has her covered." He stepped in front of her, holding out his hand. "Dance with me?"

She placed her hand in his. After all, she couldn't refuse. Nor did she wish to. Even though she'd been avoiding him all day. He led her to an empty corner of the dance floor and enfolded her into his arms. She leaned her cheek into his chest. Not only to feel him but also to avoid eye contact. Mac wasn't stupid. He'd know she was freaking out.

"You're very quiet tonight."

"Is it a problem?"

"No, it's an observation. I know this can't be easy for you.

Talk to me."

And she almost did. She wanted to. Wanted to tell him if one more person approached her, remarking on what a cute couple they made, she might punch them. But he didn't deserve it. He hadn't done anything wrong. So, she lied. "Just tired, I guess. It's been a long week."

He murmured an agreement, more sound than words. His chest rumbled against her ear.

"Ladies and gentlemen, if I could have your attention for just a moment."

She startled at the DJ's voice booming through speakers next to them. She used it as an excuse to pull away from him, put some distance between them.

"It's time," the DJ continued. The opening notes of Beyoncé's "All the Single Ladies" filled the room. "That's right, if you're single and a lady, come on out here to the dance floor."

Her eyes darted around the room, seeking an escape. But before she could make good on her plan, she felt hands on her back, propelling her forward. "Let's do this!" cried her friend Jamie in her ear. Short of making a scene, Amy was stuck. She allowed herself to be pulled along with the wave of their single friends crowding the small dance floor. Ducking to the back, she closed her eyes and wished for the bouquet to land anywhere but near her.

Paige, gorgeous in her mother's gown, approached the DJ, a huge smile on her face. Amy watched as the man whispered something in her ear, making her laugh.

"Do we have everyone?" Guests murmured and glanced around the room. "Okay, here we go. Your lovely bride is going to toss her bouquet. And you know what comes next! One lucky young, single woman will be getting a garter placed on her leg. And, as legend tells us, be the next to get married.

A chorus of laughs and nervous giggles sounded from the group of gathered women. The sound echoed through her head like a thousand bass drums. *Please let this end already.*

"Are we ready? Then let's do this on the count of three. One. Two. Three."

By the time he counted two, Amy had already stopped breathing. Every muscle in her body clenched, leaving her a statue in a sea of grasping, excited women. Anywhere but here is where she wished to be with every fiber of her being. She held her arms at her side, stiff with her hands balled into fists.

And then the bouquet hit her square in the chest. Amy reached for it without thinking. Her hands clenched the wrapped stems even as she wished she could toss it to some smiling woman who actually wanted to catch it.

"Sorry, ladies, looks like Amy Windsor, our lovely maid of honor, is the lucky winner. Now if y'all could clear the floor, let's bring up the bride and groom."

Amy bolted from the dance floor, still clutching the bouquet. She found a secluded spot near a wall to watch Quinn remove Paige's garter. Even from this distance, she could see a pretty blush spread across her friend's face. Amy didn't know if it was from Quinn's hands under her wedding dress or the suggestive music being played by the DJ. She backed up to the wall, until the reassuring weight of it kept her upright.

A loud cheer arose from the crowd. Quinn stood, twirling the navy garter around one finger. Something blue. He helped his bride from the dance floor as the DJ took over once again.

"It's Raining Men" blared throughout the room. She watched as the floor filled with men. They came in all ages, shapes, and sizes, from Donovan's and Nora's son Kieran, who attended Chapel Hill, to Mr. Sommers, the retired pharmacist who had to be pushing ninety. But she only had eyes for one. The tallest one with fiery red hair and a glint in his emerald eyes. Mac stood in the middle of the crowd, surrounded by others jockeying for position. As if he felt the weight of her stare, he turned his head toward her and winked. Her stomach plummeted. She needed air.

Amy sought the door leading to a balcony. The frigid

blast of winter night air cooled her overheated skin. She dragged in gulps of air. She would get through this. She had to. She owed Paige at least this much. But the second she could, she'd escape from this place. Escape the thoughts of things that could never be.

She closed the door in time to see Quinn saunter to the front of the dance floor. He said something she didn't catch. Something to set the group of men off in a round of catcalls and laughter. She closed her eyes as the music swelled. *Please don't let Mac catch it.*

She should have known better. She opened her eyes just as the garter sailed above everyone's head, landing right in Mac's outstretched hand as though guided by a missile. She grabbed the back of the nearest chair for support before her buckling knees gave out entirely. Her reprieve was short lived.

Wilds cheers were drowned out by "Legs" by ZZ Top. She realty hated this DJ, even though he was only doing his job. Knowing what came next, Amy straightened and started for the dance floor. A chair, recently vacated by Paige, sat waiting for her. And there stood Mac, a huge smile on his handsome face. She plastered on what she hoped passed for a smile and took her seat.

Members of the crowd formed a semicircle around them. She heard shouts of 'Guess we know who's next!' 'What a lovely couple.' Mac kneeled before her. He gazed into her eyes. "I've got you," he whispered to her before reaching for the hem of her long dress.

Without thought, her hands sought the bottom of her chair, clenching it until her knuckles ached. She sat very still, didn't speak to him or look at the others gathered. She couldn't. Every shallow breath burned. This should be her wedding. Hers and Andrew's. The one they never got to have.

Loud, ridiculous music evocative of bad porn blared through the room. Mac must have noticed something was off. He didn't play to the crowd, just rushed through the whole thing. When it ended, and everyone cheered and whistled, she shot up from the chair. He reached out to steady her, whispering to her.

"I've got you, Amy. You're okay."

But it couldn't have been further from the truth. Nothing about this night was okay. She wasn't okay and feared she might never be. The room felt smaller, more crowded, hotter. She had to escape.

"I can't do this anymore, Mac."

"Luckily, there's only one garter."

She knew he was joking, trying to lighten the mood. Trying to avoid the conversation she dreaded. She wished she could let him. But tonight had been too much. She couldn't do this again. "I think you know what I mean."

He stood very still next to her, seemingly not breathing. "I think I do. But I don't know why."

"I can't risk being hurt again. Not by you. Or anyone. I'm sorry."

She turned to leave but felt the lightest pressure of one hand on her wrist. Not restraining her. Not stopping her. More like asking her to make a choice. She pulled away until she felt his hand drop off her. "I'm sorry," she whispered before running off the dance floor. She continued to run, at least as well as she could in her delicate sandals, until she reached the coat check. Gathering her things, she fled the building.

And all the way home, she drove on auto pilot, staring straight ahead. Even now, when her heart felt like pieces of shattered glass in her chest, she remained dry-eyed. Maybe she'd never be able to cry again.

She didn't remember the drive home. Letting herself into her condo, Amy went straight to her bathroom. She stripped off her dress and pulled the hundred pins holding up the heavy curtain of her hair. When she found and removed the last one, she scrubbed her face free of the elaborate makeup. Not feeling any better, she pulled on her oldest, most comfortable flannel pajamas and raided the fridge. In the freezer, behind a row of healthy, frozen meals, sat her target.

Ben & Jerry's Brownie Batter Core ice cream. Only there for desperate situations. A harsh laugh ripped from her throat. She'd thrown away a decent man who only wanted to care for her. Yep, desperate times. She grabbed a spoon and the pint and headed to the couch.

And she almost made it, but a knock on the door stopped her. She placed them down on the coffee table and walked to the door. Dread deadened her steps. She couldn't face him again. Not after what she'd done. She peeked through the peep hole, and there he stood, all male delight, in his tuxedo. She noticed the tie was missing.

"I know you're in there, Amy. Let me in." She heard what sounded like a sigh. "Please."

Knowing she owed him at least that, she opened the door. When he came in and closed the door, he faced her, standing there until she looked up at him. "I've already said I'm sorry."

"Yes, I got that part. I have a question for you. Why have you never called me Travis?"

She'd steeled herself for what he might ask. Waited to hear him ask her to explain why. This was much worse. "I, uh, don't understand the question."

"Everyone in the world, except you, called him A.J. You called him Andrew. Why?"

"Because I don't care for nicknames. I always called him Andrew."

"Exactly. Yet from the very first, you've always called me Mac. Not Travis. Why?"

"I don't know," she whispered. Even though she did.

He took one step closer to her, not quite touching, but close enough to force her to look up at him. "I think you do know, Amy. Tell me."

He was right. She wouldn't lie to him again. "I called you Mac to keep you at a distance. Calling you by your name, calling you Travis, makes it more personal. I couldn't risk it."

She watched the hope die in his eyes. "Thanks for being honest."

He left before she could say anything else. She didn't

bother going to her bedroom. Just returned the couch and picked up the ice cream. And waited for the long night to pass.

Chapter Twenty-Four

Amy opened her door to a tanned and smiling Paige. She squeezed her best friend as hard as she could, careful to avoid the growing baby bump. "Wow. Honeymooning sure agrees with you. Come on in."

Paige entered, carrying a few brightly colored bags. "Marriage agrees with me. The honeymoon was a bonus." She wagged her eyebrows, laughing as she did.

"Quinn's secret cruise worked out then?"

"Yes, indeed We got a couple's massage. Can you even imagine Quinn doing that?"

She shook her head. "No, I cannot. Tell me he stopped at a mani/pedi. I might have to pull his man card if not," she joked.

"Any more man, and I might have died."

"Ewww. I do not need to know about the details. What's in the bags?"

Paige laughed as she dropped into the couch. "I wondered when you'd notice. Let me show you." She looked in each, biting her lower lip. "Not sure where to start."

"Did you buy out the Caribbean?" She shook her head. "You know you didn't have to get me anything. Not to mention several anythings."

"I know. It's what makes it fun. And you're fun to buy

for. Let's start here." She pulled a long, rectangular box out of one bag and presented it to Amy. "I hope you like it."

Amy laughed. "For someone who goes through life wearing flip flops and T-shirts, you have amazing taste for others. I'm sure I'll love it." She untied the bright green bow and opened the box. "How cute!" Lifting up the bracelet from its nest of cotton, she held up the charm bracelet to inspect closer. "This is super cute. Look at all the beachy things on here. I love it." She held out her wrist toward Paige. "Put it on me, please."

She fastened it before handing over another, larger box. "The bracelet was easy and looks fabulous on you. This took more thought."

"Then I can't wait to see what's inside." This time, she undid tropical wrapping paper. "I know you didn't wrap this yourself," she joked.

"I most certainly did not. I got smart and took the saleswoman up on her offer to do it. You know when I wrap it looks like a preschooler did it."

Amy laughed. "Sad but true." She ripped into the paper and opened the box. Inside, wrapped in a layer of coral tissue paper, she found a pile of brightly colored silk. Shaking it out, she oohed and aahed at the scarf. The tropical print featured birds in a riot of colors. She tied it around her neck, getting up to look in the mirror. "I love it!" hugging Paige, she sat back on the couch. "You really didn't have to. But I'm glad you did."

Paige picked up one more, small bag and handed it to her. "Here, last one."

"Honestly, you shouldn't have. This is too much, honey."

A sheen of tears coated her eyes. Paige sniffed. "I'm so thankful to have you, well, back. And if I want to buy you gifts, then I will." She wiped her nose on a tissue, her watery smile brightening her face.

"And I'm very glad to be back." She reached out and squeezed Paige's hand. "You have no idea what you mean to me. Okay, one more gift. Let me see what you got me."

She unwrapped a small, square box. Inside, she found a pair of earrings with a stone falling somewhere between blue and purple. "Oh, Amy, these are gorgeous." She started to take out the earrings she already wore.

"Hey, I've never seen those before. Where did you get them?"

Her hand stalled midway to her ear. "I, uh, got them for Christmas." Her hands shook, and she lowered them to her lap.

"Really? I don't remember seeing them on Christmas morning. Did your mom get them for you?"

"No, Mac did," she answered in a shaky voice. She'd worn them every day since the night of Paige's wedding. She wasn't sure why. Having the constant reminder of him tortured her. And yet, wearing them connected her to him. "I'm a mess."

"Honey, what's wrong?" Paige slid over on the couch until she was right next to her. "Did y'all have a fight?"

"I'm what's wrong. That man, that perfect man, was nothing but kind and gentle with me. Patient, understanding. And I threw it all away out of fear." She buried her face in her hands, not wanting to face her best friend.

"I don't know what happened. Please tell me."

She did. Every last ridiculous detail. "He wanted to dance with me, and I freaked out. Everyone kept saying things at the reception. 'What a lovely couple you make.' 'How nice it is to see you in a relationship again.' I couldn't take it. We just got started. I have no idea what I'm doing. I'm afraid all of the time. And every time someone said something to me, I shrank back a little further. Then the whole garter debacle pushed me over the edge. And I ran. Literally."

"In those heels?"

She burst into laughter. "Yes, Paige, in those skinny heels. Because I was so afraid."

"How did I not know this?"

"Paige, it was your wedding. And then you left the next day on your honeymoon. And don't you think you've wasted enough time because of me? I was going to ruin your wedding, too."

Paige's sharp intake of breath should have warned her. The other woman sat up straight, staring at her. "Let me be clear. I never 'wasted' any time on you. You are my best friend. You're my sister. And I would have wanted to help you."

She shook her head. "I know it and believe me I am very appreciative. But I had to figure this out on my own. And you had a honeymoon to get to."

Paige smiled. "Well, I'm back now. Have you figured anything out?"

"I miss Mac."

"That's a fabulous start. Do you miss him enough to take a chance on him? To tempt the universe? To risk your heart? Because there aren't any guarantees."

"I know. More than most. And I'm not sure."

"And how will you know?"

"No idea. All I do know is I miss him. A lot." She dropped her head and took in a few shallow breaths. "I love him," she whispered. Almost as though afraid to put the words out into the atmosphere. Yet the words brought a warmth to the frozen tundra of her chest, warmed it. Melted the ice encasing her heart since losing Andrew.

"It's not enough to love him."

Those words brought up her head. "What?" Not what she expected her perpetually happy, optimistic friend to say.

"Loving Mac is a great start. But you have to be sure. You now I love you, and I would do anything for you. But I love him, too. He's like the big brother I never had. Please don't hurt him. Or yourself. You can't say anything to him until you know."

"How will I know?" Her mind spun in circles trying to figure out what had happened.

Paige shrugged her shoulders. "I don't have a clue. You have to figure it out on your own. I love you both. If he ever hurt you, I might break his jaw. But I can't have you hurting him either."

"I'd never want to hurt him. You're right. He deserves better."

"Travis Mac Gregor is a good man. He cares deeply for the people in his life. I've seen it ever since Quinn and I got together. He's single because he hasn't met the right one yet. I think, hope, the one is you. But only if you're sure, Amy. Only if you're willing to risk everything." She stood then, gathering her purse and coat. "I have to get home. School starts again in the morning, and I am not ready." She covered a huge yawn with her hand, then rubbed her belly. "This little person needs a nap. Me too."

Amy walked her to the door, hugging her before she stepped outside. "Thank you, as always. You're here when I need you. I love you."

"Well, as you've pointed out, you don't love me for my fashion sense. And I'm always here for you. Always." She waved and walked to her car.

Amy went back into her condo and sat on the couch. Curling her feet under her, she stared at the dancing flames in the fireplace. She did love him. And she missed him. A lot. For days, she'd pick up her phone, wanting to call him. Wanting to hear his voice. Wanting to tell him how sorry she was. But she didn't. What would she say? He was much braver than she. She used to be brave. She used to be fearless. But losing Andrew had knocked it right out of her, leaving a pale version of herself in its wake.

She dragged a hand through her long hair. Why couldn't she take the risk? He loved her. She was sure of it. And yet, was it enough? He might not be a firefighter like Andrew, but Mac probably found himself in difficult situations at work. What if she lost him, too? Could she risk her heart? Again?

Knowing she wouldn't find the answers she needed today, Amy curled up on the couch, pulling the old afghan down over her. She closed her eyes, hoping a nap might bring her some clarity.

*****

Across town, Mac tried, without a lot of luck, to ignore his partner's weighty stare. She'd been quiet the past few shifts, looking like she wanted to talk to him about something but not saying anything. It was scary. Trina wasn't one to hold her tongue. Ever.

He sighed and got off the couch. Maybe if he went into another room, he could avoid her.

But she had other plans. The tiny woman, weighing all of one hundred and ten pounds with her gear belt on, stood in his path. "Where do you think you're going?"

He raised one brow. "To check the truck. If you don't mind."

"Have I ever left a truck in anything but perfect condition?" She tapped one, tiny booted foot.

"Uh, no. Night shift will be here soon. I thought I'd make sure."

"Sit." She pointed to the kitchen table. "Please."

"Okayyyyy." He had an idea what was coming and dreaded it. But she was his partner. And friend. So, he sat.

"This crap has gotta stop."

He didn't bother asking what crap. "I'm sorry."

And the fight went out of her. Trina's shoulder sank. "It's not about you being sorry. I'm worried about you."

He'd have preferred anger over this. "I know you are. I'm fine." Her snort stopped him in his tracks. "I'll be fine."

"What did that woman do to you?"

"Don't blame Amy."

"Give me one good reason not to. And don't you dare say A.J."

"What other reason is there? She loved him, Trina. As in wanted to get married and start a family. And he felt the same. And then some dirt bag with gasoline and a mountain of debt took it all away from them. From her."

"I get it. I do. But we lost him, too. As harsh as this sounds, life goes on. Or it should."

"I agree, but then I'm not the one who ended things. I can't make her love me, Trina. I can't make her risk having her heart broken again. It's her choice to make."

"Can I punch her? I'd feel better if I could punch her."

Laughter snorted out of him. "No, you may not punch her. I love her. With all my heart. I don't want to see her hurt in any way."

"And what now?"

"I go back to doing what I do. Living my life. I'll be fine." His hearty tone didn't hide his sadness. Not from her or himself. He could only hope the words proved true in the end.

"Well, this sucks. I want to fix this for you."

"I know you do. And I love you for it. But it's not going to happen." The outer door opened, followed by the hearty noise of two male voices. "Looks like our relief is here."

"You're sure I can't punch her?"

"Yes, I'm sure."

"Fine. But the offer stands."

"I know." He leaned down and kissed her dark hair, grateful for such a friend.

*****

Amy juggled two bags of groceries, her phone, purse and keys while she unlocked the door.

"Hey," came a voice from her left, startling her enough to lose the balancing act. Apples and other assorted food spilled from the bags as she dropped them. She turned to see Trina, Mac's partner, standing on the porch.

"Oh. I didn't see you when I walked up. Sorry."

"My bad. Didn't mean to startle you." The younger woman leaned down, helping to gather the wayward groceries.

"Thanks. Do you want to come in?"

"Sure. If you have a minute."

"Of course." She led the way into the common hallway and then opened her condo door. Once inside, she took the bags from Trina. "Can I get you anything?"

"I want to punch you, but my softy partner said no."

"Excuse me?"

To her surprise, the other woman grinned. "Sorry. Mac's always saying how I lack a filter." She sighed. "He's my partner. And even though I already have several, he's my big brother as well. And he's hurting. Because of you."

"Oh." She tried to not smile. The other woman might be all hard-core on the outside, but she obviously cared for Mac. "I am sorry."

"Ugh. I wanted to hate you. At least not like you." She leaned in closer, peering up at Amy, and whistled. "Are those the earrings he got you for Christmas?"

She didn't have to touch them to know. "Yes, they are."

"Nice." She cleared her throat. "I didn't come to talk about jewelry."

Amy held up a hand, stopping the other woman in her tracks. "Please know I never meant to hurt him. He's special."

"You got that, huh?"

"I did."

"Then what gives? You obviously care about him. And he, uh, cares about you, too."

"It's not so simple for me."

"Of course, it isn't," she replied in a tone implying Trina didn't think much of her intelligence. "It's never simple. My husband makes me crazy. Not a week goes by when I don't think about connecting a frying pan to his head. But I love him. Can't imagine life without him."

"Imagine losing all that. Losing him. Then someone comes along who makes you want it again."

"Oh."

"Exactly. It's not that I don't care about him. But I don't want to, can't actually, go through it again. I simply cannot."

"But what's the alternative? Being alone? Never loving anyone again? A.J. thought you hung the moon. He wouldn't want this for you."

"Don't you think I know?" she all but whispered. Her

throat grew heavy, making speech difficult.

Trina put her arms around Amy, hugging her. "I'm sorry. I shouldn't have come here. I didn't mean to make it worse for you." She released her, stepping back. "Please don't mention this to him. I meant well. Really."

"Of course not. This can be our little secret. And please believe me. I want to trust it again. Take the leap. More than you could possibly imagine."

"I'm going to go now. Thanks for listening to me. Sorry I scared you." She let herself out.

Of course, Mac would have people in his life who loved him so much. She smiled at the thought. From what she'd seen of him, Mac inspired loyalty in others. Love. Respect. In a lot of ways, the important ways, he reminded her of Andrew. Although the day was a huge painful blur for her, Amy remembered the sense of loss, the grief for their beloved friend and colleague.

She put the kettle on and waited for the water to boil. Glancing around her home, she tried to see it through other's eyes. It seemed sterile. All touches of Andrew long gone. Kind of like her life. Trina had a point. Did she really want to live this way? And then she thought of Mac. His warm smile lighting his clear, green eyes. His hearty laugh starting in his belly. His kindness toward her when she'd been a shrew to him.

She might be playing it safe. Hiding here in her home. Venturing out when she felt strong enough to do so. But what about him? All he'd done was listened to her. Comforted her. Befriended her. Loved her. Mac didn't deserve her treatment. He deserved better. So, did she.

The kettle whistled as the smile grew on her face. She knew what she had to do. Now to figure out how.

Chapter Twenty-Five

Mac pulled on the tight bow tie for the millionth time in the past hour. "This is ridiculous," he grumbled. "Why do I have to wear a tux? Again."

"Someone has to look good out there, since I'm off the market." Quinn held up his left hand to prove his point. His silver wedding band shone in the overhead lights.

"Very funny." Mac continued to fuss with his tie, trying to center it.

"Come on now. It's for charity. The new pediatric oncology wing at the medical center needs a lot of toys for the kids who will fill the beds."

"Not to mention things like a CT scanner. Those 'toys' come with a hefty price tag."

"And there's your fear of Mrs. Windsor."

"I am not afraid of her." He turned to face the mirror, making sure the damned tie sat straight.

"Are, too," Quinn replied.

"What are you six?" Giving up on the tie, Mac turned from the mirror

"Just calling it like I see it."

He grinned. Yep, they sounded like a bunch of kids. "Whatever. But for the record, I am not afraid of Susan Windsor." He crossed his fingers, knowing he was a bit intimidated by the older woman.

"Says you." Quinn grinned at him before peeking out at the packed ballroom. "Looks like Jack's up. You're next. Need anything?"

"An escape route?"

Both men laughed then stopped and listened. Loud cheering, maybe even a wolf whistle, came from behind the curtain. Mac swallowed hard. This was so much harder than he reckoned when he volunteered. 'I introduce you. Then they bid, and you go on a date. It's all for fun and a very good cause.' At least that's what Amy's mother had told him. There hadn't been any mention of wolf whistles. He wiped his damp palms on his trousers.

The clear sound of a gavel slamming preceded a round of cheering.

"My turn I guess."

"Good luck out there, man. And watch out for old lady Schwartz. She's very handsy." Quinn ducked out a side door leading to the ballroom, his laughter lingering in the air.

"Great." Mac knew all about Mrs. Schwartz. The woman had to be in her eighties. Rich as hell from nobody knew what, she was often the center of Windsor Falls gossip.

He heard his name called. His cue to meet his fate. Mac slid between the edges of the heavy, velvet curtain, plastering a huge smile on his face. He'd agreed to this. Might as well do it right.

Jack passed him on his way off the stage. "Twenty-five hundred, baby. Good luck beating that!"

Months ago, when both men had been voluntold by Mrs. Windsor for this gig, Jack had bragged about earning more money. Never one to back down, Mac had taken the bet. Unless he wanted to wash the other man's car for a whole year, he better beat the price.

"Good evening, ladies!" he yelled as he strode on the stage. "Who's feeling lucky, and generous, tonight?"

A rousing cheer went up with a bid of two hundred yelled from somewhere in the back. Blinded by the spotlights, he had no idea who yelled it.

The gavel sounded. "All right, ladies, let me introduce Travis 'Mac' Mac Gregor. Mac is another of our local heroes. He's a paramedic. That's right, he can get your heart started right up again. Mac loves to play golf in the summer and ski in the winter. Who'd like to go on a date with Mac? Now, since we've already had a bid of two hundred, which is very low in my humble opinion, let's start there. Do I hear three hundred?"

"Three fifty," yelled a suspiciously old sounding voice from up front.

Mac squinted, trying to see better. He'd recognize the sixty-year, two-packs-a-day voice anywhere. Mrs. Schwartz. He unbuttoned his tux jacket and strutted over to the podium. "Surely, I'm worth more than this, ladies?"

Another round of catcalls and whistles, far louder than the last, rose from the crowd. He tried to ignore the heat spreading across his face.

"One thousand."

"Now that's more like it," responded Mrs. Windsor. She glanced down at the front. "Do I hear two?"

"Three thousand," rasped the octogenarian.

Mac swallowed. Hard. No one was going to top three thousand. At least he won the bet with Jack. Having the cocky firefighter wash his car would be worth it. He hoped.

"Three thousand down front. Do I hear Thirty-five hundred?" She waited a moment, glancing around the room.

Please! Mac froze his smile. The money was for a good cause. How bad could one night be?

"You're almost mine," croaked Mrs. Schwartz before erupting in a coughing fit.

Sweat broke out on Mac's forehead. He contemplated making his own bid.

"Going once. Going twice."

Think of the kids, he reminded himself.

"Going."

"Ten thousand dollars!"

For a moment, those words hung in the air. No one spoke. He was afraid to move a muscle. Had he heard right? Someone was willing to pay ten thousand for a date with him? Why?

"Well, it seems we have ourselves a new highest bidder. Do I hear ten five?"

He stood very still, refusing to look in Mrs. Schwartz's direction. But he prayed hard. *Please don't top it!* He had no idea who had bid such a ridiculous amount of money for him, but she had to be better than Old Handsy Schwartz.

No one else called out a bid.

"Going once. Going Twice." Mrs. Windsor paused, probably for dramatic effect, but all it did was send his heart rate into triple digits. Sweat trickled down the center of his back.

"Sold! To the very eager young woman in the back."

Mac saw someone stand and walk toward the stage. As the figure approached, his heart raced. But for a different reason altogether. Wearing the enticing silver gown from Paige's wedding, Amy approached the stage, with a huge smile on her face and tears running down her cheeks. Tears! He'd never seen her cry. Not once in all the conversations they'd had about A.J. He rushed toward her.

"What's wrong?"

"I thought I'd lost you. I feared losing again, being hurt, so much so I shut myself off from you. But all I did was hurt myself. And you." In her heels, she stood almost on eye level with him. "I'm really sorry, Travis."

His heart thumped in his chest so hard he thought it might have somersaulted. "Amy, are you sure?"

She nodded, trying to wipe the tears now flowing freely down her face. "I'm scared. Really scared. But I missed you. A lot."

He stepped in close, oblivious to the suddenly silent crowd. "I know." He wiped a finger under each eye. "It's okay to be scared, Amy. I'm right here." He took her hand and placed it over his heart. "I'm not going anywhere."

She smiled then. And the sadness of the past few weeks vanished. "I know you are. I need you to be a bit patient. Give me time. Because I love you, Travis."

And he did the only thing a smart man could. He kissed her. In front of her mother. In front of hundreds of people. Mac leaned in and kissed her. And then he whispered against her lips, "Welcome back."

The End

Epilogue

The warm April sun shone on Amy as she exited Travis's truck. "Are you ready for this?" she joked. "It's kind of a big commitment."

"More than ready," he replied before kissing her until he took her breath. After a moment, he came up for air.

"Then let's do this. You know, Gus is going to love having a brother."

"Or sister. I'm open to either."

She took his hand as they approached the animal shelter door. A cacophony of canine voices greeted them, bringing a smile to her face.

ACKNOWLEDGMENTS

This is the last book in my Windsor Falls series; the end of an era. It's bittersweet for me. This is my very first series, so letting go is not the easiest thing I've ever done. But I think it's time.

Writing Amy's story means so much to me. She'd suffered such a devastating loss in *Saving Quinn*. And so, I wrote and wrote. Had more than 15K finished when my Mom died in July of 2018. And I found myself in a hotel room in Scranton, PA trying to write about grief, while I was living it. I closed the document, and the Addie Foster Series was born. Writing really is cheaper than therapy... I started up again in November, when I felt I was ready to handle it. And I wrote and wrote again. Until my laptop crashed. You guessed it; hadn't saved it correctly. I lost over 10K. I'm much better at backing things up now in case you were wondering. So, thank you to all the wonderful readers who have hung on, waiting for Amy's story. I hope you'll be pleased.

Thank you to the amazing Jeni Burns, who kicked my butt a bit on this one. You were right. There, I said it. And if anyone cries reading this book, it's all her fault.

Margie Greenhow, my overworked but very appreciated PA, keeps me on track and sane (relatively) through this long process. Thank you for all you do!

What can you say about the cover artist who gives you exactly what you wanted when you weren't really sure yourself? Kudos to Rebecca Pau of The Final Wrap for creating these brilliant covers. Every time.

New to my team is the wonderful Chelly Hoyle Peeler, my new proofer and formatter. Welcome aboard, Chelly!!!

WHAT'S NEXT?

At some point in the future, I will start my next contemporary series set in Serenity Bay, NC. Think Oak Island for those of you familiar... Remember Bailey from *Second Chances?* I'll be starting with her story, finding love again as she runs her B&B, Sunrise House, in Serenity Bay. And if some of the characters from my Windsor Falls series appear along the way, all the better.

Made in the
USA
Columbia, SC